THE CAPTAIN'S BRIDE

Orphan Tabitha, running away from her scheming grandmother, naively encounters problems which land her in gaol. Transportation follows, and the harsh conditions onboard the convict ship are lessened when she impresses the captain. Jacob contacts his friend in Australia, asking if he and his wife can offer Tabitha a job. Their mutual attraction develops. After their marriage, the captain decides to abandon seafaring and open a school, helped by his young bride. Will Tabitha's harsh beginning have a happy ending?

THE CAPTAIN'S BRIDE

Orphan Tabitha, running away from her scheming grandmother, naively encounters problems which land her in gaol. Transportation follows, and the harsh conditions onboard the convict ship are lessened when she impresses the captain. Jacob contacts his friend in Australia, asking if he and his wife can offer Tabitha a job. Their mutual attraction develops. After their marriage, the captain decides to abandon seafaring and open a school, helped by his young bride. Will Tabitha's harsh beginning have a happy ending?

JILL BARRY

◆

THE CAPTAIN'S BRIDE

Complete and Unabridged

LINFORD
Leicester

First published in Great Britain in 2021

First Linford Edition
published 2022

Copyright © 2021 by DC Thomson & Co. Ltd.,
and Jill Barry

A catalogue record for this book is available
from the British Library.

ISBN 978–1–4448–4821–2

Published by
Ulverscroft Limited
Anstey, Leicestershire

Printed and bound in Great Britain by
TJ Books Ltd., Padstow, Cornwall

This book is printed on acid-free paper

Lancashire 1861

'Stay in this house? How will you pay the rent, lass?' Margaret Entwistle drew her grey woollen shawl more tightly around her and looked pityingly at her sixteen-year-old granddaughter.

'Are you sure my father didn't leave me any money?' Tabitha saw the look on her grandmother's face and her spirits plummeted even lower.

'I checked under the mattress, amongst other places, while you were getting that shopping for me.' Mrs Entwistle frowned.

'We all knew your father was hopeless at saving for a rainy day. He couldn't understand how short-sighted he was, helping other folks when you were barely managing.' She sighed and Tabitha knew it was with impatience, not sympathy.

'Aye,' her grandmother continued, 'my son-in-law was a proud man and wouldn't ever accept my help, God rest his soul.

'I'm sorry for your loss, Tabitha, but you need to fetch your things and come home with me. There's nothing to keep you in Rockham.' She sniffed. 'Not a town I've ever warmed to.'

Tabitha was trying her hardest not to cry in front of this forbidding old lady.

She had very few memories of her own mother. But she clearly recalled a sweet voice singing a lullaby when she was tucked up in bed ... a smiling face and unruly bright curls just like her own mop of hair.

But she knew, from things her father said, her mother was a gentle soul, nothing like the stern matriarch now glaring at her. But though she might wish to remain in her own home, she knew when she was beaten. She was an orphan and needed to accept her situation.

She fled upstairs to her room, where she pulled an old carpet bag from beneath the bed and began stuffing a few possessions inside. In went the black-covered bible from beneath her pillow, closely followed by a yellow-haired rag doll, which her mother had made. Tabitha always felt there was much love stitched into little Maisie.

She stripped the bed of its bedraggled sheets and blankets, folding them carefully on the mattress before taking one final look round and going, her heart a solid lump of misery in her chest, back to her grandmother.

Margaret Entwistle opened the door and called to the elderly manservant waiting with the pony and trap.

'We're ready now, Mr Yates.' She turned to Tabitha. 'In you get and don't you go looking back. Look to the future.'

Tabitha climbed up and settled into the far corner. Her grandmother, still sprightly for her sixty or so years, accepted a little help from Mr Yates and sat beside her, remaining silent, as though sensing her granddaughter needed time to adjust to her changed circumstances.

They drove down narrow streets, houses crammed higgledy-piggledy, many of them with children playing outside. Some of them stared and pointed, their shouts and laughter echoing in Tabitha's ears while the chestnut pony clip-clopped along, pulling the two-wheeled shiny black carriage over ruts and potholes.

After a while, the jolting and the heady scent of jasmine oil which her grandmother wore like an extra layer of clothing, made Tabitha feel queasy. She closed her eyes, wishing she was anywhere but here, sitting beside a woman she didn't totally trust, let alone love. But where else could she go?

She could hardly ask her grandmother if there were other relations who might accept her. And even if there were, no doubt they'd regard her as a hussy, like her mother before her.

* * *

'Tabitha? We're almost there!'

She opened her eyes to find they were in the midst of trees and fields with an occasional barn. Her mother, Elizabeth, was brought up here, but Tabitha barely remembered those few visits she'd made.

'It's a pity your father didn't allow you to see me, Tabitha, after your mother died. Never mind, we can make up for that now, can't we? Rest assured I have plans for you, child. Tell me, is that the only shawl you possess?'

'It is, ma'am.'

Her grandmother muttered something inaudible. She wondered what plans the old lady meant, but didn't risk enquiring.

They'd turned off the road now and ahead lay the house.

She knew her grandma had done her best to prevent Elizabeth from marrying Tabitha's father, and suspected this was the reason why he became withdrawn over the years, eking out a living by taking odd jobs.

At twelve, Tabitha had found work in a local candle factory and though the tasks were tedious and the foreman stern, her fellow workers showed kindness to a motherless girl.

She wondered how long it would take to replace her when she didn't arrive come Monday morning.

'Tabitha Westwood! My, but you're a daydreamer. Just like your mother before you!'

Tabitha gathered herself together. Mr Yates was helping her grandmother descend from the carriage. When she was safely down, he took Tabitha's bag from her, gripping her arm as her feet, seemingly unwilling to carry her, caused her to stumble.

'I'm sorry for your loss, Miss West-wood,' he said. Tabitha thought his voice sounded rich but croaky, like thick molasses with gravel. But she kept this thought to herself.

Her grandmother was already at the front door, looking impatient.

'Come, child,' she called. 'These damp afternoons don't suit my delicate consti-tution.'

Safely inside with the door closed behind her, Tabitha looked around. This wasn't a vast, extravagant house, but the furniture, heavy velvet curtains and the pictures adorning the walls confirmed what she already knew.

How sad that her mother, by running away to marry the man she loved, lived in poverty until pneumonia had its cruel way with her.

'Pinkerton! Where are you? Come here at once!'

Tabitha jumped, startled out of her musings. As if she'd been waiting in the wings, a tiny woman dressed entirely in black, scuttled from nowhere like a small woodland creature trying to avoid predators.

'I'm sorry, Mrs Entwistle.'

'Pinkerton, this is my granddaughter. As you know, Tabitha is to sleep in the old nursery. You shall show her the room and help her move things round to her liking, but first I think we should take tea.

'Kindly ask Alice to provide a tray for three. Has she made cake in my absence? Yesterday's jam sponge was good for nothing but trifle!'

Abruptly, she moved across the hallway and through an open door, closing it behind her.

Tabitha found herself hoping the person called Alice had done as she was bid. Maybe the cook would be less forbidding than these other two women.

She looked at Mrs Pinkerton, not encouraged by the way her lips were clamped together as if glued. Maybe it would be wise to try and get on her right side?

And did having to move into this household mean she was regarded as a family member or a servant? No doubt she was about to find out.

Shock Announcement

'Wait here, if you please.' Pinkerton disappeared through a door which led, presumably, to the kitchen.

Curious, Tabitha looked around, feeling awed by her surroundings. This mightn't be a nobleman's residence, but it was bigger than even the parsonage she'd visited, let alone the cottage her father had been renting. Their tiny scullery would fit into this hallway a dozen times!

But how she wished to be back in Dents Row, with neighbours who often squabbled and shouted but who she could turn to in time of need. They'd done their best to help when her father grew weaker, but he had too much against him to recover.

Despite everyone telling her she must make a new life, she felt helpless with her grandma in control. Penniless, she would be at the old lady's beck and call. It was difficult to imagine her own mother as a small child, clinging to Margaret Entwistle's skirts.

Maybe Tabitha was being unfair. Perhaps the years since seeing her only daughter disobey her and marry someone who worked as a gardener, not a banker or lawyer, had been difficult for her, too.

Glancing up at the staircase, Tabitha's heartbeat quickened on noticing a familiar face. A sunbeam highlighted the image, inviting attention. Surely that young girl in the portrait could only be her mother? She almost tripped over her carpet bag, so eager was she to move closer.

She stopped on the landing, gazing at the figure in the white organdie party dress, as though wanting to step through the picture frame and embrace her.

'I'm not here to wait on you, missy!'

Tabitha scuttled back down and grabbed the offending bag. Pinkerton stood, her podgy little hands clasped before her.

'I beg your pardon, Mrs Pinkerton. My attention was caught by that picture. Please believe I never took you for a servant. You look far too important.' How her father would laugh if he could hear her now!

'Yes, well, my official title is companion to your grandmother.' She looked up at Tabitha, who towered over her. 'Now, let us go upstairs so you know where you'll be sleeping.'

But Tabitha realised her rather grovelling remark had gone down well. She followed her guide upstairs and across a wide landing with a corridor leading off. Pinkerton trotted on until she reached the door at the end. She thrust it open and stood back while Tabitha carried her bag inside.

'Oh, my!' All of a sudden Tabitha felt a strange sensation. Still shocked and saddened at losing her father, it hadn't occurred to her the nursery, now allocated as her bedroom, might contain items associated with her late mother.

The wallpaper was blue and white.

The curtains were faded pink velvet. On the window-sill sat a small collection of dolls. Here she was, gazing at her mother's past and suddenly it all became too much to bear. Tears streamed down her cheeks and she made no effort to stem them.

'What is it?' Pinkerton was looking at her in surprise. 'Ah, I see,' she exclaimed, before taking her bag and handing her a large white handkerchief.

'I'm sorry,' she said gruffly. 'Dear me! Your grandmother should have thought about this before.'

Tabitha tried to pull herself together, feeling better now she knew Pinkerton possessed a streak of human kindness.

'It's all right,' she said. 'I should have realised when my grandmother mentioned where I'd be sleeping.'

'We can arrange things later. Your grandmother hates to be kept waiting.'

Tabitha brushed down her skirt, pleased to see no signs of mud on the hem, and smoothed down her curls, using both hands.

'Why not use your mother's hairbrush? It's where she left it.' Pinkerton pointed to the dressing table.

Tabitha picked up the silver-backed brush. The precious metal shone, with no signs of tarnishing.

'Who keeps the room looking so well? There's no sign of dust and this brush is gleaming.' She raised it, tidying her hair while watching her reflection in the mirror.

'Alice and I take turns. You remind me very much of your mother ... but we must make haste so not to keep Mrs Entwistle waiting.'

'I... I didn't know you knew my ma.' Tabitha replaced the brush and followed the little woman from the room.

'I never met her. I answered Mrs Entwistle's advertisement for a companion housekeeper and at that time your grandmother was alone here, except for Mr Yates in the gardener's cottage.

'But I've seen likenesses of Elizabeth, of course. Your grandparents must have been very proud of their only daughter.'

'Until she displeased them by running away to get married!' Tabitha knew she shouldn't be gossiping about her own kin, but Pinkerton seemed to be warming to her and she didn't want to appear standoffish.

'I dare say she had her reasons.'

By the tone of Mrs Pinkerton's voice, Tabitha knew this conversation was at an end.

They hurried downstairs and into the parlour where Margaret Entwistle sat in a winged armchair, her spine straight as the ebony-topped cane she'd used when she came to collect Tabitha.

She waved to the settee opposite and Pinkerton began pouring tea into rose-splashed china cups, the finest Tabitha had ever seen.

'Sit opposite me so I can see you. I'd like you to read to me later. You can read, I suppose?'

'Yes, Grandma.'

'I imagine your mother taught you? Or did you go to school before your father lost his money? Remind me how many years old you are!'

Tabitha's hands were clasped in her lap but this cruel comment caused her to squeeze her fingers together. She held the old lady's gaze.

'I've reached sixteen years and six months and, yes, my mother taught me to read. My other grandma used to tell me about foreign countries and their different languages and wild creatures.'

'Did she indeed? And where is she now, may I ask?'

Tabitha bowed her head.

'She's gone to be with her maker.'

The elderly lady didn't respond, except to harrumph a bit and shift in her chair. Tabitha sipped her tea, secretly enjoying having silenced her grandmother, if only temporarily. She eyed the cake greedily. How long was it since her last meal?

Pinkerton came to her rescue by putting a slice upon a plate and placing it before her. Tabitha looked up.

'Thank you,' she whispered.

'Now then,' Margaret Entwistle picked up her cup, 'we need to prepare you for your new life. You're a mite scrawny for a gentlewoman, so Alice's pastry pies and beef and bone stew will be the making of you. How long since you took a bath?'

'Um...' Tabitha couldn't remember the last time she cleansed herself except by washing at the kitchen sink. And she'd never once considered herself as a gentlewoman.

'No matter. Tomorrow you shall bathe and we shall purchase clothes for you. I have a plan for your future but you're not, as yet, ready to meet the gentleman to whom I've decided you will become betrothed. Your life is about to be transformed.'

Tabitha's mouth was crammed with sweet, delicious, sticky fruit cake. This household didn't stint on food, it seemed.

But her mind was still replaying the sadness of the last few days and she wasn't fully concentrating on what her grandmother was saying. But both women were staring at her, awaiting, she supposed, a response.

Something about being prepared to

meet a gentleman ... become a companion to some widowed gentleman's children, perhaps? That mightn't be so bad. Children meant the possibility of love, laughter and fun, didn't they?

'I'm so sorry, Grandma. You mentioned a gentleman?'

'Wake up, child, and heed what I say, if you please! Once I'm satisfied you are ready to meet the gentleman I have in mind, you'll be presented to him.

'Edgar Kershaw is a clergyman — a kindly widower who is childless. He will make you an eminently suitable husband.' Tabitha's grandmother smiled, though her next comment was chilling.

'I consider you to be just the young woman Edgar needs to help him achieve the large family to which he aspires.'

Escape Plan

Silence reigned as all three concentrated upon their tea and cake. Tabitha was hungry, yet how could she eat now? The tick-tock of the mantelpiece clock might as well have been signalling a prison sentence. Yet her grandmother appeared unaware of her discomfort, moving swiftly on to clothing needs, followed by a speech outlining the many faults she had identified in Tabitha's father.

His daughter found it difficult to sit there without protesting. Why would a Christian woman wish to speak ill of the dead? But when she glanced at Pinkerton, the dutiful little person gave a slight shake of the head.

A warning? Tabitha thought so, and although longing to protest her fate, knew better than to antagonise Margaret Entwistle before having spent even one night beneath her roof.

She understood better now, how her mother must have agonised over her startling decision to run away. Had Elizabeth also been shocked to discover a suitable match was arranged for her?

If so, no wonder she decided to run to the man she loved. Although she longed to, Tabitha daren't enquire about this clergyman she was supposed to marry.

What age was he? How was his disposition? And how soon would she be obliged to wed him? She didn't feel ready for marriage. Indeed, the prospect terrified her. As for children …

Tabitha had been brought up as a God-fearing girl who said her prayers at night and who often read the bible which used to belong to her mother. She would pray for deliverance from the destiny chosen for her.

But after only a brief acquaintance with her grandmother, and from snippets gleaned from Pinkerton, she feared this mightn't prove as easy as she might hope.

Her grandma insisted she read aloud

from 'Gulliver's Travels' but after a while, Tabitha noticed the old lady's eyelids drooping and her chin dropping to her chest.

Another glance at Pinkerton prompted a nod of approval this time, so she continued reading in her low, clear voice, until her grandma suddenly sat upright and barked, 'Enough!' followed by a grudging, 'You read well.'

Supper was baked ham with vegetables followed by custard tart, taken in the dining-room though the lady of the house complained of the chilly atmosphere. Pinkerton offered to light the fire already set for the morning.

'D'you think I'm made of money, woman?' the old lady snapped.

Tabitha kept her head bent over her food, speaking only when spoken to, still contemplating the fate awaiting her.

If only she'd known, she would somehow have escaped her grandmother's clutches, exactly as her mother did. She was certain she could have taken refuge at her place of work, but it was too late now.

Yet, a fledgling idea was sparking inside her head, a notion so daring and so unlike her, she almost felt like laughing at the sheer impudence of it.

She didn't, of course, allow herself to fall into that trap. Nor would she say anything to Pinkerton, or to plump, homely Alice, who she'd met before supper. Although she felt sure each of these women would understand her dismay, it was safer to act as though everything was fine.

* * *

Next morning, after a night disturbed by dreams of a masked horseman trying to scoop her up and ride away with her, Tabitha took a bath in a wooden tub kept in the laundry room. Alice poured in the water and helped wash her hair, handing her a cloth to wrap around her head afterwards.

To her surprise, Pinkerton had already visited a local clothes dealer and returned

21

with garments for her to try on. This convinced Tabitha of her grandmother's standing within the area but depressed her by making her feel she'd no choice in the matter. Her opinions weren't worth a bone button and she'd best get used to it.

Back in her room, after putting on the chemise and neat grey dress selected for her, sounds from below sent her to the window.

A horse and carriage stood on the driveway below, while Mr Yates, the elderly gardener, made haste across the lawn to help the occupant exit the carriage. Mr Yates led the horse away while a portly gentleman approached the front door.

Tabitha noted his sombre suit and clerical collar. Could this be the clergyman her grandma mentioned? Surely not! Looking at the gentleman's wispy grey hair escaping from his hat and his pale complexion, Tabitha, whose knowledge of men was limited, reckoned this one must have reached the age of forty.

He couldn't be Edgar Kershaw — of that she was certain.

Someone, probably Pinkerton, opened the door and the caller removed his headgear, bowed and disappeared from view. Because of his clothes and his beaky nose, he reminded Tabitha of a large black crow, a dismaying image which was to haunt her for a very long time.

She crept downstairs to the kitchen and found Alice preparing a tray of tea.

'My grandmother has a visitor, I see.'

Alice frowned.

'Aye, it's fortunate there's cake in the larder because he has a sweet tooth, does our vicar.'

Tabitha froze.

'That gentleman is Mr Kershaw? But he is so very old!'

The cook chuckled.

'To you, maybe, Miss Tabitha. He doesn't seem as such to me.'

'Alice, please call me Tabitha. You've been so kind to me, even in the short time I've been here.'

Alice nodded.

'When we're alone, then. I wish you were staying longer than a few months, my dear. It's like a breath of fresh air, having you here. Now, would you like to take this tray into the parlour?'

Tabitha hesitated. Would Margaret Entwistle be furious if her charge suddenly appeared? Maybe the clergyman would take an instant dislike to his prospective bride? Oh, if only! She was still hovering when Pinkerton arrived.

'Tray's ready, Mrs Pinkerton,' Alice said. 'Miss Tabitha was just about to bring it in.'

'No need, Alice, thank you. I'll take it. Tabitha, best you don't interrupt your grandmother while she's talking to her visitor.' Pinkerton picked up the tray and headed for the door. Tabitha darted ahead to open it wider and was graced with a small smile.

How she longed to protest at the unfairness of all this, especially now she'd seen the man who would be her husband. She was even more determined to avoid her fate and all the more convinced she daren't confide in either Alice or Pinkerton.

* * *

After the midday meal, during which Tabitha found it difficult to making polite conversation, Margaret Entwistle, who according to Alice had enjoyed a couple of glasses of Madeira wine with the clergyman, made it clear she intended taking a rest.

'You may continue with our reading at four o'clock,' she said.

'Yes, Grandmother.' Tabitha hid her glee.

This was the perfect opportunity, though she must take care not to cause noise, or attract suspicion. Knowing which room her late grandfather had used, she intended searching for garments to help achieve her escape plan.

She'd asked Alice what build of man her grandfather had been, holding her breath when the older woman described him as short in stature with a slight frame. He'd spent much time with Yates in the garden and enjoyed walking. Alice called him a kindly man, who was devastated when his only daughter left home.

Tabitha's plan depended upon her getting hold of masculine attire. She feared, unless disguised, setting off by herself would prove hazardous. A lone boy, travelling to the nearest large town, surely wouldn't cause comment? And if her grandfather liked being outdoors, she'd surely find suitable clothing?

Once upstairs, Tabitha crept along the corridor, pausing outside her grandma's bedroom. Hearing the faint but regular sound of snoring encouraged her to walk on to the room she required. Would her luck hold? Breathing a sigh of relief that the room wasn't locked, she entered, closing the door quietly after her.

She tiptoed across the faded carpet to the wardrobe. The door swung open to reveal jackets, trousers and a formal suit, but at the wardrobe's base were two sturdy drawers. Tabitha knelt down and helped herself to a few items before returning to her room.

* * *

A couple of nights later, Tabitha hardly dared sleep when the household retired. She'd been afraid to tackle Margaret Entwistle on the subject of marriage, fearing she might be confined to her room.

Escaping seemed the only option and now the time had come. She needed to quit the house next morning, before even Alice stirred. She thanked her lucky stars this was the month of May and the weather had been kindly.

As dawn approached, she quickly pulled on the long-sleeved shirt and trousers, securing them with a silken rope purloined from her grandfather's dressing gown. His old jacket felt slack across her shoulders but she felt it likely for a humble lad to be kitted out with hand-me-downs.

In her old carpet bag, Tabitha placed

her bible, the precious handmade doll, and a purse containing a little money. She planned to help herself to bread, cheese and fruit from the pantry before leaving.

She'd no idea what drove her grandmother to matchmake with such disastrous results. To Tabitha, the portly clergyman was someone she could never warm to. He must find someone else to be the mother of his children.

Mission accomplished, she hurried down the driveway. Once through the gate, she breathed a sigh of relief. She had already decided to try for work as a bottle boy in an inn or, if she saw a similar residence to her grandmother's, she might enquire if they needed extra help.

But neither option could be contemplated until she'd travelled a considerable number of miles.

Tabitha walked and walked, watching the sun climb higher in the sky. Passing through a small hamlet, she stopped at a pump to ease her thirst. Realising an old woman was watching her from across the way, she gave her a friendly wave and set off again, whistling cheerfully. She still hadn't travelled far enough to enquire about odd jobs and didn't allow herself to dwell upon what might happen if she was unsuccessful.

Dangerous Situation

Counting the milestones was becoming less fun now. Tabitha, almost dragging her feet, longed for somewhere to rest. Her heart seemed to skip a beat as she saw she was nearing the boundary of a village five miles from Danton, her final destination.

Seated on the grass beside the highway, she glanced up at the sound of hooves clattering on the dusty road. A rider on a black horse was cantering towards her. Her stomach lurched as she recalled her worrying dream about the dark horseman, but to her surprise, the rider was leading a second horse, a pretty chestnut.

'Whoa there, Topper!'

Tabitha shrank back as he dismounted and led both horses towards her. But remembering her boyish guise, she held her head high, trying to look as if she possessed all the confidence in the world.

'Hey up!' The man sported a beard and wore his hair in a tail, fastened behind his neck. To Tabitha's relief, his gaze was friendly.

She got to her feet, running a hand through her hair. She'd hacked off most of it the night before, for fear of appearing too feminine. Now she nodded to the stranger, waiting for him to speak.

'Heading for the city, lad?'

'Yes, sir.' She felt satisfied with the gruffness of her tone.

'Strikes me we could do one another a favour if you ride the chestnut, young sir. What d'you think?'

Tabitha was temporarily speechless.

'Well, can you handle a horse or not?'

She hadn't had much experience but the opportunity to reach Danton more quickly than she could on foot was too tempting to refuse.

'I can, sir. I accept your offer with thanks.'

'Joe Cullen at your service.'

Her heart pounded so fast, she almost

introduced herself by her own name.

'Billy Walsh, sir,' she said. It was the first name that popped into her head.

'We'll ride into the village, Billy, see if we can find refreshment then head for Danton. I'd as soon be there by nightfall. Let me tie that bag of yours to my saddle, then I'll give you a leg up. Bess is a placid mare and shouldn't give you any trouble.'

'I'm indebted to you, sir.'

'Joe to you, my young friend.'

Tabitha could barely believe her luck. Although she felt stiff-legged and awkward at first, she soon slipped into the horse's natural rhythm and began to enjoy the ride.

Joe didn't say much, didn't question her about her journey and for that she felt thankful and in turn didn't query his business.

* * *

They reached the city boundary as twilight softened the landscape and the evening chill made Tabitha glad of her grandfather's warm jacket, shabby though it was. She was relieved to spot an inn sign up ahead and sure enough, Joe called to her to head round to the yard.

She wondered whether, if she offered to do some washing up, the innkeeper would give her some scraps of food and a drink of the local ale. But her companion surprised her as he dismounted and she followed suit.

'I doubt you have the coins to pay for your supper, Billy, so I'll treat you to it, on one condition.'

'What's that?' She held her breath.

'I have dealings the other side of the city so must leave early in the morning. I have a fancy to give you a chance in life — such chances are few and far between for the likes of us, so I'm going to let you take Bess.' He raised his hand to stop her protest. 'You can't afford to feed yourself let alone feed the mare, so you need to take her to market tomorrow and sell her.'

Tabitha couldn't believe he meant what he said.

'I can't let you do that!'

'You can and you must. I don't like the thought of you wandering around on your own. With money in your pocket, you can pay for lodgings and find work.

'You're a handsome lad and bright enough to get taken on as an apprentice or an office clerk. Now, let's get the horses stabled, order food, then see if the landlord has room for two weary travellers.'

* * *

Morning light filtered through the grubby window, telling her someone must have opened the shutters. Tabitha raised herself on one elbow, and seeing the pallet Joe had slept on was empty, scrambled to her feet, untied the twine she'd used to fasten her bag to her ankle, and left the room where several other travellers still slept.

In the yard she splashed water from

the pump over her hands and face and went to talk to one of the lads. She prayed he'd help her saddle up Bess, doubting she could manage it alone. A tow-headed boy of about twelve years came to her rescue and she was on her way. Following directions Joe gave her, Tabitha rode through the streets until she reached her destination. Here she saw traders unloading their goods from carts and barrows and she called out to one of them, asking the way to the horse fair.

'You'll need to ride on, lad!' A plump fellow stopped work and peered at her. 'Keep going till you get to the field at the end. You'll see the traders but you'll have to trust to luck you find a fair 'un.'

Tabitha thanked him and urged the mare on, suddenly realising she'd miss her placid Bess, but she needed money to make a new life.

If only her grandmother hadn't decided to marry her off! Living under the old lady's guardianship, she may have found work as a companion or even governess to a family with young children. But she faced a very different future now and needed to keep her wits about her.

Tabitha stroked Bess's neck and dismounted. One or two of the traders were lounging nearby and she knew they were discussing her. Did they suspect? If her disguise should be penetrated... Her mouth dried, wondering how on earth she'd manage this situation. But Joe had told her the kind of money she should ask for and that provided the shred of confidence she needed. She led Bess forward and nodded to the two men.

'That's a fine mare you have there, young fellow.' The taller of the two stood, hands on hips, surveying Bess's appearance.

'Aye, and she has a good nature, too.' Tabitha was acutely conscious of her shabby appearance. If only she'd been able to borrow garments that didn't make her look quite so poverty-stricken! But she hadn't wanted to attract attention and so far, that had worked. Now, she dreaded being questioned as to how she came by the horse. What if they didn't believe her?

'Tether her to the post while we take stock. How much were you looking to get?' The second man was examining the mare's mouth. Once Tabitha's trembling fingers had tethered her, he picked up one of Bess's back legs and inspected her hoof.

'Easy, girl,' he said.

Tabitha felt a surge of hope. Could she possibly pull this off?

Both men were silent, each of them hovering beside the horse. They kept their voices low, so as not to startle her, Tabitha reckoned, but it also meant she couldn't hear what they said. Then the shorter of the two turned to face her.

'I need advice. If you stay here with Will, I'll not be long.'

Tabitha inclined her head. To her relief, Will appeared unwilling to make conversation. Instead, he strolled off to stand a few yards away. Good sign or bad? She'd no idea. This new world she'd entered was unknown and frightening. Yet, the thought of having money in her pocket, enabling her to purchase new clothing and return to being a girl, spurred her on.

After all, if she fled the market now, where else could she go? Without coins in her pocket, both she and Bess would starve. Tabitha straightened her back and folded her arms, trying not to think of her grandma's good food and comfortable house.

Will's companion was walking back. Grim-faced, he strode across the field, heading straight for Tabitha. She sucked in her breath. Following him was a man dressed befitting some official position. Should she run? Or should she stay? The decision was made for her as she realised her feet were as if frozen to the turf beneath.

What Fate Awaits?

How could she have been so trusting — so stupid? Tabitha sat huddled on the floor of a dingy dungeon, frightened and chilly. Somehow, she still retained her bag though she feared someone older and bigger would probably find a way of snatching it. Dark depression surrounded her.

Joe Cullen had given her a stolen mare! She'd never even thought there might be such a thing as a register of horses in the county. Never once imagined Joe might be a horse thief.

Why, oh why had she accepted the kind stranger's offer? Of course, she'd been weary and ravenous, her judgement less sharp than it should have been, but she'd been swift to agree and now suffered the consequences.

She closed her eyes, feeling the sting of salty tears, and lowered her head to rest on her knees as she hugged them, rocking back and forth in the deepest despair she'd ever experienced.

After a while, she raised her head, rubbing her eyes and sniffing. Luckily, her surroundings didn't smell too bad. Her throat dried as she saw a movement over in the corner by the door. After being shoved roughly into this dank and cheerless prison, she hadn't noticed she had company. Now she feared the other occupant might jeer at her for shedding tears, especially if he happened to be male.

'Hello. I'm Jenny.'

Tabitha felt a wave of relief. Maybe her fellow prisoner hadn't noticed her show of despair. In her hurry to introduce herself she stammered as she almost revealed her real name. She really must be more careful.

'I'm Billy. How long have you been here?' Tabitha wondered if her voice sounded gruff enough but Jenny didn't seem suspicious.

'Since last night,' her cell-mate said.

'I think I must've been fast asleep when they brung you in.' She put her head on one side. 'Hey, you ain't murdered no-one, have you?'

Tabitha shook her head.

'Not me. I've been taken for a fool, that's why I'm in here. How about you?'

'I helped myself to my mistress's silk handkerchiefs. Only took two, but I reckon someone went in my room to see what they could nick. They must've noticed the hankies and gone straight to the mistress. She didn't take long to get me reported and stuck in here.'

Tabitha couldn't hide her soft heart.

'That's awful. I bet you did it because you were desperate for money?'

Jenny nodded.

'Aye. Ma's got five little 'uns at home and a second husband what drinks. I only wanted to flog the hankies and give my ma the money.'

'I'm so sorry.'

But Jenny looked fierce.

'No good us being sorry, mate. We're stuck here now with worse to come. Who

41

made a fool outa you then?'

'A stranger who took pity on me — a man who turned out to be a horse thief. He offered to give me one of his horses so I could sell it at market and I was daft enough to accept. No self-respecting livestock dealer would believe a scruffy lad could own such a beautiful mare.'

Jenny's mouth was open.

'You talk like a toff but you don't look like one.'

'That's because I'm not.' Tabitha needed to change the subject away from her background. 'I... I ran away from home because my grandma had plans for me that I didn't fancy.' She could have kicked herself for revealing the truth instead of telling Jenny any old rubbish that came into her head.

'But was it a nice home? Did ya get enough to eat?'

'I was well fed, yes.'

'Huh! Then more fool you fer not heeding the old biddy! What did she want to do with you?'

Tabitha thought swiftly.

42

'Um, she wanted to send me off to some foreign country. I don't know which, but she has a cousin out there who runs some kind of plantation.'

'All I can say is, you must be dafter than you looks. Sounds to me like you'd 'ave been on to a good thing there, Billy, me darlin'. Funny thing is, you're gonna get over the water all right. But as a prisoner, not as a well-heeled young fella!'

Tabitha stared at her companion, horrified.

'Wha … what do you mean, Jenny?'

The girl pulled a face and rubbed her hand over her mouth.

'I'm gonna yell fer water and vittles if nobody brings 'em soon. Now, what do you think I mean? That's a hanging offence you got there, Billy boy. You got to hope they lets you choose between the noose and transportation.'

'Transportation where?'

'Where d'you think? Why, Australia, of course. I'll be sent there, that's for sure. Now all you can do is pray.'

Next day, Tabitha and Jenny learned

they were to be moved. Tabitha was to be sent to Newgate Prison and Jenny to Bridewell. More and more alarmed now, Tabitha sought frantically for some way of avoiding this. She'd been pleased with her disguise, but now found the thought of being locked up with so many men really frightening.

Jenny noticed her anxiety and lost no time in putting her halfpennyworth in — one of her favourite expressions.

''Ere, what's the matter, mate? Do you know something I don't?'

'Yes.' She heaved a sigh. 'You see ... I'm not who you think I am.'

'Garn! You're a prince in disguise and you've sent a message to your father to send soldiers to rescue you! Take me with you, Billy boy!' She rocked back and forth, laughing.

Tabitha took a deep breath and spoke in her normal voice.

'I'm a girl, not a boy. My name's Tabitha.'

Jenny fell silent.

'How come you're dressed in men's

clobber, then?'

'Because I thought pretending to be a boy would stop me getting noticed but then that horse thief put paid to any chance of my making my own way in life.'

'By jiminy, there's a surprise! Cross me heart and hope to die, I never guessed. But y'know they'll find out, don't you? Once you're stuck in Newgate, you'll not last long among all them rough fellows.

'You have to tell them now, Billy — Tabitha. Just tell 'em why you did it, like you told me. Then we'll both be sent to Bridewell.'

Tabitha bit her lip and though she tried hard, she couldn't stop the tears trickling down her cheeks. Jenny got up and put her arms around her.

'We'll be sisters. Look out for one another. That all right with you?'

Tabitha brushed away the tears and nodded.

'Yes. Let's do that.' But she hadn't forgotten Jenny's warning about the noose. And she didn't think admitting to being

a woman would make the authorities any
more forgiving about her fate.

★ ★ ★

Tabitha, having confessed her true iden-
tity, had been sent to Bridewell as Jenny
prophesied.

She'd lost count of the days that had
passed since her one and only visit to
the bathtub at her grandma's house.
Fleetingly she wondered what Margaret
Entwistle would say if she knew where
her charge was now. She hoped Pinkerton wasn't suffering from ill humour on
her grandma's part. Mrs Entwistle must
be furious because Tabitha chose to disobey her, just as her daughter Elizabeth
had done.

Even so, panic gripped her as she realised there was no way back. No matter
how much she'd dreaded the prospect
of becoming wedded to a man she knew
she could never love, she now felt she'd
exchanged one awful fate for another.

This new development would take her

far away from England and into a completely new world. Yet, no matter how frightened she was, at least she was still alive. She'd protested her innocence, but those in charge, although deciding this young convict didn't warrant the death penalty, still issued the transportation order.

Tabitha held out her arms to receive the clothing bundle presented to her by a jailoress.

'Get those on and go next door for your meal. And mind you don't try no funny tricks! The only place you're going is Blackfriars Bridge, and that's a fact. Rather you than me, little miss!'

Tabitha scuttled back to her corner, firstly pulling on undergarments, then a smock made of coarse fabric. She'd no idea what the weather was like in Australia but was glad of the shawl and sturdy boots.

Nor had she any idea what had become of her carpet bag, not that she now had need of male clothing. But she hated the thought of being parted from those precious souvenirs of life with her parents.

'You! Through here now.'

Tabitha found herself in a hall where women sat at trestle tables. Bowls of what looked like broth were being served. She joined the small queue and looked around for Jenny, feeling a rush of relief as she spotted the dark-haired girl at a table with space opposite her.

She took her bowl and a chunk of bread then carried the food carefully across the room, determined to get there before one of the wardens ordered her to take the nearest empty place.

Jenny grinned as Tabitha placed her bowl on the table and began gnawing the bread.

'I wondered if you'd turn up. So, this means you escaped the noose?' She gave a loud, throaty laugh.

'Shush,' Tabitha said. 'I don't want any more attention if I can help it.'

Jenny leaned forward.

'You gave me such a shock. I'm glad, though. I meant what I said about us being like sisters.'

'I know you did.' Tabitha began on her broth, which didn't taste too bad. 'It was true what I said about my grandma. I knew I could never do what she wanted.'

'You never told me what she were really planning.'

'If you must know, she wanted to marry me off to the local clergyman.'

Jenny stopped spooning broth into her mouth.

'But you'd have been set up fer life, you numbskull! What I wouldn't give for such a chance …'

'You wouldn't say that if you'd seen him!'

The two locked gazes and suddenly each began to giggle. A jailoress walked across and clamped a meaty hand on Tabitha's shoulder.

'Up you get. Take your bowl and sit somewhere else.'

'We're doing no harm,' Jenny muttered.

The woman scowled and wagged her finger in Jenny's face.

'Oh, please!' Tabitha got to her feet. 'It

was my fault for making her laugh.'

'Oh, whatever you say, your highness!' The older woman looked contemptuously at Tabitha. 'You'll be laughing on the other side of your face before long. Now, get on your way before you annoy me any more.'

Journey Into the Unknown

Tabitha waited her turn to get on the next carriage. This would take her to Blackfriars Bridge where the convicts would embark on a ship known as *The Lady Gwendoline*, which would sail to the New World she'd heard people talk about. It seemed some saw that continent as a personal kind of hell while others viewed it as somewhere to make a fresh start.

Tabitha preferred the second option, but a long, arduous voyage lay ahead before she discovered what life had in store next.

She jumped as someone pushed her from behind.

'Get a move on, dearie. Anyone'd think you didn't want to go nowhere!'

Tabitha heard a cackling laugh then a sharp elbow nudged her in the ribs and she shuffled forward dutifully. Once in the carriage, jammed shoulder to shoulder with the other female convicts, Tabitha gazed at the drab London streets. Almost everyone, she noticed, was doing the same.

There was no chatter and she thought this must be because they'd all finally realised this departure was really about to happen. The day when they left familiar things behind and sailed for an unknown land, had arrived.

As the coach pulled up at the quayside, Tabitha heard some of the women murmuring to each other and craned her neck to see what was catching their attention. She saw the tall masts of a vessel and knew it must be the ship soon to become their temporary home.

Now the first of the convicts were leaving the coach, some looking wildly around as if contemplating escape. But the guards loomed, their faces grim as they shepherded the women into a line ready to board the Australia-bound vessel.

Clutching her beloved carpet bag with one hand and holding on to her shawl with the other, Tabitha walked up the gangway. There were plainly dressed women on deck, chivvying the new arrivals and escorting them below deck.

Ahead of her, women were being herded towards a gangway leading into the depths of the vessel. Would the prisoners not be allowed to stay on deck for a while and enjoy the fresh air? Was there no clemency in this world in which she now found herself? She hadn't seen Jenny since the pair were ordered to board different coaches. You're on your own, Tabitha, she told herself.

* * *

Captain Jacob Learman heaved a sigh of satisfaction as his ship left its mooring at the appointed time. At the wheel, he watched familiar landmarks appear then slide into the distance as *The Lady Gwendoline* forged her way through the Thames estuary towards the North Sea.

Jacob had always wanted to see the world. He'd served his apprenticeship from his tenth birthday through the years until his thirtieth. His seafaring friends gradually became more like family, something which he greatly valued, as neither of his parents was still alive.

His only brother lived in London and, several years older than Jacob, had a wife and four children. He visited them occasionally when his voyages permitted.

But for the last couple of years, he'd envied his brother and wondered how he could possibly meet a suitable young lady and win her hand when he was away from England so much.

His dilemma ended when one of his friends, another captain, found Jacob was not only in London between ships in late December, but had no plans for Christmas Day.

'Good heavens, man,' George had said, 'you must come to my humble abode and meet my family.'

Jacob accepted the invitation gratefully, totally unaware he'd be seated at luncheon next to George's sister-in-law, a young woman of twenty or so years.

He feared Caroline would be bored with him — another seafaring man, as unlikely to entertain her with tales of parties and balls as her brother-in-law George would be!

But Jacob and Caroline discovered a mutual love of music and at the end of the celebrations, he was enquiring whether she had any admirers or whether he might be permitted to call upon her next day.

He smiled to himself as he remembered how her face lit up and how her sister, George's wife, had conveniently ignored the rules of etiquette and taken the children out for half an hour, leaving the young couple to become better acquainted.

He'd liked the way Caroline's blue eyes sparkled. He'd noticed how the scent of lavender clung to the silky folds of her gown.

Months later, between voyages, Jacob talked himself into asking for her hand in marriage before taking over his next ship and leaving for the coast of south-eastern

Australia. However, illness in the family prevented him from visiting George's residence. The womenfolk and children were in strict quarantine and, with time against him, Jacob decided to write a letter to Caroline after his ship sailed and ensure it was posted at the next port of call. She was a sweet girl, polite and good with her young nieces and nephews.

Jacob longed for children of his own and though he knew he wasn't head over heels in love, he was extremely fond of her. And he was well aware his lifestyle wasn't the most secure in the world. Not only was the sea an unpredictable workplace, but many young ladies wouldn't relish the prospect of being left husbandless for months on end. He felt this particular one would probably take it in her stride.

The pilot was preparing to leave the ship. Jacob shook the man's hand and thanked him. They exchanged a few words before the fellow wished him a good voyage and left the bridge. Jacob squared his shoulders and gazed into the distance as his crew members went about their duties. He frowned as he realised it was time to show his face on deck.

'Take over, Robert. I shan't be long.'

Jacob left his second-in-command in charge and headed for the main deck. Here he saw the usual scene — yet, he frowned as someone caught his eye. He stopped in his tracks. A slight young woman, huddled into her grey woollen shawl, stood gazing out at the water.

Jacob frowned. What was this all about?

He cleared his throat. The young woman whirled round to face him. She staggered slightly and Jacob reached out both hands to hold her firmly but gently by the shoulders. A lock of hair, the colour of molten copper, peeped from beneath her sturdy cap. A pair of brown eyes beneath shapely brows met the captain's gaze.

At that moment, he knew his life would be for ever linked with hers. He banished this ridiculous notion from his mind.

'What are you doing here, child? Why are you not below with the others?'

He marvelled at the way she held his gaze. No shiftiness, no stammered excuse.

'I'm very sorry, sir, but I'm no child!' She bit her lip. 'I wanted to take a last look at Blackfriars Bridge as the ship took sail.' She spoke clearly and Jacob realised this was no street urchin.

He released her shoulders.

'How old are you?'

'I have sixteen years and seven months, sir.'

'Have you indeed?' He smiled. 'Do you know who I am? Don't be afraid — you're not in any trouble.'

Her smile was a joy to behold, her teeth surprisingly white. What on earth could this young woman have done to warrant banishment to the other side of the world?

'Beg pardon, sir, but by your uniform and bearing, I believe you're the ship's master.'

'I am indeed. Captain Jacob Learman

at your service. And you are…?'

'Tabitha Westwood, sir.'

Jacob glanced towards the companionway leading to the prison deck. He felt surprisingly reluctant to consign this girl to her quarters. There was something about her that intrigued him, but he'd no other option. He beckoned to one of the women who helped with the female captives.

'My apologies, mistress. I detained this young woman on deck in order to discover something of her background.'

Tabitha's eyes widened in surprise.

'Take her below, if you please.'

Jacob watched young Tabitha Westwood curtsey then walk away. Hours later, when he put pen to paper to write to his intended, he was puzzled by an image of brown eyes and copper curls appearing in his mind. Didn't the woman he wanted to marry possess blue eyes and golden hair?

Unexpected Opportunity

'Tabby! What kept ya?'

Tabitha was relieved to hear Jenny's voice as she picked her way between lines of hammocks.

'I've been up on deck. Couldn't see you anywhere!' She headed for her friend.

'How'd you manage not to get spotted?'

'I was in a quiet corner of the deck then the captain happened by and he kept me talking.'

'Blimey! You don't waste no time, do ya? And now you're blushing! Is he nice?'

'He's very polite. A real gentleman and he wanted to know a little about me.' Tabitha tried not to sound as though she'd received any favouritism.

'Well, I've been saving this hammock next to mine, hoping you'd come in here.' Jenny's heart-shaped face split into a wicked grin. 'I've had to pretend I was waiting for my sister!'

Tabitha gasped.

'I'm pleased to have found you, but won't the custodians wonder why we have different names?'

'Don't worry. We ain't going nowhere in a hurry and we need to stick together,' Jenny said. 'Watch each other's back and make sure to keep out of trouble.'

'Seems to me we're in enough of that already!'

Tabitha looked around her, wondering what different crimes all these women were guilty of. Was horse theft regarded as the most scandalous offence of all? It was far more serious than stealing brass buttons or bread rolls. Would anyone besides Jenny believe she'd been duped by a scoundrel?

Many of their fellow-prisoners were lying in their hammocks. Some were sobbing. Others lay on their backs, their expressions blank as they stared at the wooden rafters above. No doubt each of them had a tale to tell.

At that moment Tabitha wondered how on earth she'd manage to pass the forthcoming days, weeks and months of this dismal voyage. She had a book or two in her bag. Would there be books on board for those who could read?

Jenny reached out a hand and squeezed her shoulder.

'We've got one another. And thank your lucky stars you ain't got to wed that fat parson your grandma had up her sleeve!'

Tabitha giggled. No-one knew what the future held, but they were young and full of energy. And hope. Everyone needed hope. She resolved to thank the good Lord when she said her prayers before she went to sleep. Thank him for sparing her and for giving her the chance to forge a new life.

Two of the custodians were moving amongst the hammocks, asking questions of some occupants, ignoring others. The taller of the two pushed her way through and stood between the two girls. She looked curiously at Tabitha.

'Name?'

'Tabitha Westwood, ma'am.'

The woman's finger moved down her list. 'The horse thief.' She met Tabitha's gaze. 'How'd you manage to pull that off — a young wench like you?'

'Please, I ... I was given that pretty mare. I'm no horse thief, truly I'm not!'

The woman pursed her lips.

'And I'm Queen Victoria!' She chortled. 'Take my advice, Miss Hoity-Toity, and keep your trap shut. That way you won't tell lies!'

Tabitha knew it was pointless arguing. The custodian smirked and moved on, ignoring Jenny.

Tabitha thought about the ship's master who'd come across her earlier. If she ever got the chance to explain how she'd been wrongly convicted, would he believe her? Or would he laugh in her face? But she doubted their paths would meet again. He was the captain who must be obeyed by everyone. She was nothing but a lowly convict.

* * *

The next few days passed slowly as the women tried to settle in to their new life. There were some whom Tabitha feared, though Jenny told her to ignore them. But Tabitha mistrusted their sly expressions as they sized up their shipmates.

All the women wore the same drab brown dresses, with shawls, stockings and boots. But some of the convicts had more possessions than others and Tabitha knew her carpet bag was gaining notice from one or two of the more experienced lawbreakers.

Each time the women were escorted up on deck for their daily exercise, she hung back so she was last to leave. With Jenny in her confidence, it was easy to ensure one or the other was first in the reluctant queue to go back afterwards.

One fine morning a week or so into the voyage, they'd returned to their quarters after exercising, when Tabitha received a visitor.

'The Master wants a word so you're

to come with me now.' The custodian pulled a face. 'No idea why, so don't bother asking.'

Tabitha thought quickly. This was her chance to take her belongings and throw herself upon Captain Learman's mercy. She feared losing those last few reminders of her beloved mother and placing them in his care would fill her with relief. She pulled the bag from beneath her hammock and stood up straight. Her escort laughed.

'You're not jumping ship, you fool. Leave that!'

'Please, mistress, I prefer to take it with me.'

The older woman stared back at her then shrugged her shoulders.

'Don't say I didn't warn you. Come on then.'

'Good luck,' Jenny whispered.

Tabitha nodded at her and followed the custodian who stalked ahead until they reached their destination. Here she tapped gently on an oak door, its panels, Tabitha noted, polished to perfection.

'Enter.'

Her escort turned the brass doorknob and gave Tabitha a push. She found herself in a pleasant cabin containing furniture and a beautiful mahogany desk at which the captain sat. He sprang to his feet immediately, making Tabitha's heart skip a beat in acknowledgment of his politeness.

'Miss Westwood, take the seat opposite me, if you please.' He turned to the custodian. 'Thank you very much, mistress. If you wait nearby, I'll call when I need you to escort this young woman back again.'

Alone with the captain, Tabitha dropped her bag on the floor, walked to the chair he indicated and seated herself. How she longed to be wearing one of the pretty dresses her mother used to make for her!

An image flashed into her mind of the market stall back in Rockham where her mother purchased material to make garments for herself and her family. Bright floral muslins, pastel cottons, sturdy material for her father's shirts, rolls of jewel-coloured velvets... She dragged herself back to the present.

Captain Learman turned over a page and looked up from the large, leather-bound notebook lying on his desk. He smiled.

'Tabitha — if I may call you that?'

She nodded, wondering what this was about. At least he didn't seem angry.

'I've a mind to put you to work.' He must have seen the alarm in her eyes. 'Oh, please don't fear — I shan't have you scrubbing the decks or scouring cooking pots!'

She managed a weak smile.

He consulted his notebook again.

'We have a young family on board, father imprisoned for stealing fruit from a market stall.' He compressed his lips. 'He was desperate to feed his family. Have you ever known hunger, Tabitha? Real hunger with no hope of being fed?'

His blue eyes were mesmerising. Something burned within him that she wouldn't have associated with a man in his position.

'Not often, sir. I can feel nothing but compassion for the man you mention.'

Jacob nodded.

'It seems you and I have been more fortunate. By the way, what do you carry in the bag you left by my door?'

She felt her throat dry.

'Please forgive me if I appear impertinent, sir, but I would much appreciate your keeping it safe for me. Within it are remembrances of my parents — such as a little doll my mother made for me. They will be of no interest to anyone but myself and yet ...'

He nodded.

'They're important to you and you fear the bag might be stolen.'

He gave a wry smile and she knew at once what she must say.

'I do. As for me — I'm no thief, Captain Learman. Never in a hundred years would I have stolen a horse.' She held her head high and gazed into his eyes. 'But if I had starving children, I might well have stolen in order to feed them.'

He still held her gaze.

'As might I, Tabitha Westwood ... as might I.'

They sat in silence for moments before he spoke again.

'The couple I mention have three children under the age of seven, one still a babe in arms. I'd like you to move into their quarters because I think you could help them through this voyage, by entertaining the two older ones — maybe assisting with the baby? It would be good experience for you in terms of future employment in your new country.'

Tabitha's first thought was of Jenny. What would her friend think? Yet, the captain awaited her answer. He was allowing Tabitha, a convicted thief, freedom of choice. She marvelled at his interest in her situation and the good intention behind his suggestion.

'I'd be honoured to join this family, sir. And I'm very grateful for your consideration. When should I begin my duties?'

Marriage Proposal

Bob and Mary Lennox were delighted to meet their new nursemaid. Mary shed a tear when Tabitha appeared. Bob placed his arm around his pretty wife's shoulders and shook Tabitha by the hand. She noted their accommodation was at the other end of the ship from the women's dormitory and felt sad at the thought of not seeing Jenny, except maybe by chance. But she rolled up her sleeves and immediately received her first lesson in caring for a baby.

'This captain's a good man.' Bob confided his thoughts to Tabitha as they were taking the children for some fresh air up on deck a day or two later.

'I told him about my desperate state when I was forced to steal food to put in the children's mouths and he was very understanding — made me feel as though I was still an honest man and not a criminal.

'He asked what my trade was and when I said I'd worked as an office clerk, he expressed surprise. I explained I'd been plotted against and a theft took place for which I was blamed. A lot of cash was stolen and my enemies copped the lot.'

Tabitha stopped walking.

'I'm so sorry! But that's like what happened to me. Except I was given a stolen horse. I still don't know how I could have been so stupid as to fall for that story.'

'Blimey, how dreadful! The wife and I wondered what a nice girl like you could've done to get herself transported. Does the captain know?'

'I mentioned it. But what could he do?'

'He might come up with something — maybe put in a word for you and say you shouldn't have been sent here in the first place.'

She swallowed hard.

'I know it might sound silly, but I think I'm better off making a new life in Australia. My parents are both dead and my grandma wanted to marry me off to someone years older. I couldn't expect Captain Learman to put himself out for me and anyway, making my own way in London would be difficult, I think.'

'I'm sorry to say it won't be easy getting on with life in Australia. But I'm prepared to work at whatever I'm given. Land's cheap, so I hear. It might take a few years, but if only Mary and me can get by, we could end up owning a nice little spread. Farming's in my blood, so who knows?'

They beamed at one another.

'And Mary tells me she used to be a seamstress before she got married,' Tabitha said.

'A good one, too. I pray she'll be able to use her skills again in the new world.'

They fell silent as the ship lurched and each of them hurriedly reached for a child. Tabitha held little Betty in her arms and sang a nursery rhyme, to stop her from whimpering.

Bobby, her elder brother, was wriggling in his father's arms, asking to be let down to play again. Then one of the women whose job it was to supervise the families, arrived to warn them it was time to return to their quarters.

Tabitha could see Mary was having a hard time with the baby when she walked in. The young mother looked tired, probably because of baby Thomas's teething problems, so Tabitha offered to tell the children a story.

'You're an angel in disguise, my dear,' Mary said as her husband gently took the wriggling infant from her arms and cuddled him against his shoulder.

'I doubt that,' Tabitha said. 'But I've plenty of stories in my head from the days when my mother used to tell them to me.'

The evening passed quietly after Thomas was fed and settled down to sleep. Tabitha was already accustomed to an early bedtime and being woken at dawn. At times she thought longingly of the last proper bath she'd taken and this was one such occasion.

She wondered, too, whether her grandmother's relationship with the local clergyman was still intact. She imagined he wouldn't wish to antagonise a patron such as Margaret Entwistle.

Drifting off to sleep, a blanket tucked around her to keep the night-time chill at bay, she wondered when, or indeed if, she'd see the captain again. Though, now he'd arranged for her new shipboard routine, she must accept there was no need for her still to remain on his mind…

* * *

Jacob had at last written his letter. He sat back in his chair and reread his words, even though he'd taken pains with them.

At sea. Tuesday 2nd April

My dear Caroline.
I trust you're in good health, also that your sister and the children are well. I expect George is at sea again by now. If your sister is writing to him, perhaps you would ask her to convey my good wishes

for his wellbeing.

All goes as well as expected on board The Lady Gwendoline. She's a favourite of mine, a vessel with particularly fine Captain's Quarters. Our ship's cook is a good fellow and rules his staff with a rod of iron.

There is evidence of the usual hardship and plights amongst the prisoners. I have knowledge of the unfairness that takes place within the judicial system. In particular I think of a man who claims to have been plotted against and blamed for the theft of a large amount of cash from the firm he worked for. There's also a young girl whose full story I do not know, but she has confessed to being duped by a rogue she met while travelling, thus taking the blame for horse theft after he gave her a stolen mare.

Believe me, my dear, I have no doubt these sad accounts are true. I have, over the years, acquired some knowledge of human nature and will do my best to ensure these two people can make a better start in the state of Victoria, than they, as convicts, might have expected.

Now to the heart of the matter, to which I've given serious consideration since our first meeting.

I didn't feel it was proper to ask the question I'm about to ask, whilst our acquaintance was still so brief. Now I (and I hope you) have had a chance to review our friendship, I trust you agree the time has come when I should make a certain declaration.

Before leaving London, I met with George to ascertain how he'd view me as a prospective brother-in-law and I'm pleased to say I met with a cordial reception. You, my dear, possess the perfect qualifications to make any man a loving, faithful wife.

As for myself, I'm no great catch, having spent so many years at sea. Yet, you have seen your sister adjust to spending time without a loving husband at her side, which is one reason why I dare approach you.

Would you, my dear Caroline, do me the honour of becoming my wife? You may, of course, wish to take time to ponder your answer. That is only fair and to be expected. I will wait to hear from you, at which point, should you consent, we perhaps could dare to select a suitable date for our betrothal to be announced and to decide upon a date for our wedding early next year or even later this year.

I shall close now, as we reach our first port of call very soon and I wish this letter to reach you without delay.

With warm regards, I remain your loving friend and suitor,
Jacob Learman

He sealed the letter carefully and placed the envelope in the middle of his desk. Rising, he walked across to the sideboard and poured a measure of port wine into a goblet. He felt relieved to have expressed his wish at last, yet didn't experience the elation he knew he should. This wasn't how a prospective bridegroom should feel, of that he was sure.

Relishing the mellow flavour of the

wine, he savoured a further swallow. This was not too bad a life, but it could be a lonely one. He needed to keep his distance from everyone bar those officers he relied upon, but he realised he was missing female company. He'd enjoyed the hours spent with Caroline whilst on his last leave. That was a good sign, wasn't it?

He shook his head in bafflement. He'd accomplished what he wanted. His match with Caroline was, he felt certain, an extremely sensible one.

Yet, why could he not put thoughts of young Tabitha Westwood from his mind? He was as good as engaged to be married and besides, she was only in her seventeenth year while he was in his thirtieth. But it wasn't as though he wanted to marry the girl! She was probably one of only a few females on board who weren't illiterate. She would probably enjoy choosing something from his small library, so why shouldn't he invite her to select a book and maybe enjoy a few minutes of conversation?

Next day, after the families took their exercise up on deck, Tabitha was singing to the children while their parents collected food for the little ones' midday meal. The baby was fast asleep in his basket.

Hearing the murmur of greetings, she looked up to find the captain approaching. He was but a few feet away when he called to her not to unsettle the children. However, both of them slid from her lap and jumped into their hammock, giggling and chattering.

At once, Tabitha rose and curtsied, just as Jacob bowed his head to her. Once again, she marvelled at the captain's manner. Bob was right. This was a man who possessed the qualities allowing him to reach the position he held, yet also to make ordinary folk feel at ease and as though they were of some worth to society.

'Tabitha. How are you faring? And do seat yourself again, please.'

'Thank you, sir.' She sat on a low stool beside the children, both of whom seemed fascinated by the visitor's smart uniform and shiny brass buttons.

'I met with Mr and Mrs Lennox when I visited the refectory.' He smiled. 'It seems they're very pleased with the new addition to their family.'

'But sir, it is I who am the lucky one. I feel useful again and it's all thanks to you.'

He inclined his head.

'I merely made a suggestion though it's gratifying when others approve. But I must move on. My reason for calling was to ask whether you'd like to borrow one of my books.'

Tabitha gasped.

'You'd really trust me with one?'

'Why not? Your parents obviously felt you should learn to read. You must be missing the joy of that, though I fear I have no romantic novels unless you count 'Little Women', which my sister-in-law insisted I should bring. There are books by Tolstoy and Dickens...'

He was looking expectantly at her. She swallowed.

'I'll read anything, sir. I have only two books with me, both of which are in your care.'

'And which you've read more than once, perhaps?'

'Indeed, sir, I have.'

'Then come to my cabin no earlier than three o'clock today and you may choose something from my small library. If any of the custodians ask what your business is, you may tell them you're obeying the captain's orders.'

'Thank you, sir.' She hesitated. 'I fear though that I cannot ensure your book's safety as I have nowhere to store it.'

'Ah, of course. Then we must make an arrangement. Unless you hear otherwise, you may present yourself at my door each afternoon at three o'clock. You can spend an hour or two reading, whether I'm there or not. I shall instruct my officers as to my wishes.'

His gaze lingered on her for moments. She was unable to prevent herself from smiling. And when he returned her smile, a little bubble of joy reminded her how lucky she was to be sailing with Captain Jacob Learman.

Then he was gone and the children were pulling at her skirts and demanding another story. Their parents arrived within moments and the attention of the little ones was focused upon their meal.

Tabitha, overjoyed by the captain's suggestion, couldn't wait for tomorrow to come.

Suspicious Minds

Jacob didn't miss the expression on his second-in-command's face when he explained he'd given permission for a female convict to spend time reading in his cabin each afternoon.

'Robert?' Jacob tapped the envelope waiting on his blotter. 'This letter includes a proposal of marriage I've written to a young lady of whom I'm very fond. Do you really think I'm the kind of man to take advantage of a young person within my care?

'I must admit to feeling disappointed if that's how I'm viewed by someone for whom I have the greatest of respect and who I know will make an admirable ship's captain one day.'

His brother officer looked highly embarrassed but pulled himself together and saluted his chief.

'I meant no offence, sir. Please forgive

me for looking sceptical. It was merely that I didn't imagine any of those female prisoners would possess the ability to read.'

'This particular young woman has more intelligence than most people would realise.

Tabitha Westwood is to be allowed inside my cabin each afternoon, even in my absence, so she may read undisturbed.'

Robert looked worried.

'But, sir? What about the artefacts and your personal possessions? Will you lock them away?'

Jacob shook his head.

'Maybe you'll tell me where a thief would stow such ill-gotten gains?'

'With respect, sir, isn't this young woman the horse thief? She was found out and thrown into prison.'

'Don't believe everything you hear, Robert. If you were to converse with Tabitha, you'd soon become aware of her character. She has been the victim of injustice and I intend to help her rise above an unfortunate situation.'

Robert bowed his head.

'Forgive my haste in jumping to con-clusions. I'll personally ensure Miss Westwood isn't intimidated or harassed in any way should you be absent when she arrives.'

'Thank you. Now shall we ring for tea? I want to discuss a weather phenomenon we might encounter upon the next stage of our voyage.'

But later, after the lamps were lit, Jacob recalled his brother officer's words. He was beginning to realise how a caring attitude towards a female convict could be misunderstood and might even cause jealousy.

He would never wish Tabitha to be sneered at or bullied in any way. He thanked his lucky stars he'd arranged to involve her with Bob and Mary Len-nox and knew the couple would protect her as they would their own flesh and blood.

★ ★ ★

Tabitha felt nervous about explaining her new afternoon routine to Bob and Mary. At first, Mary looked stricken and Tabitha realised she assumed this was some kind of punishment. She was soon reassured, although her husband was a different matter. Thunder clouds gathered as Bob scowled and clenched both fists, obviously unsure how to form the words he wanted to say.

Life had forced Tabitha to grow up quickly and she realised at once what he suspected.

'Be assured, Bob, Captain Learman's a true gentleman. He's allowing me to spend time reading so I may improve my learning. He may sometimes be elsewhere, but he's instructed his crew to allow me into his day cabin for this purpose.'

'I see.' Bob still looked concerned. 'Begging your pardon, but what good can this do you? You're a girl and you don't need learning.'

Tabitha glanced at Mary who seemed determined to look anywhere but at

Tabitha or her husband.

'I only got into this predicament because I didn't want to be married off to a man I could never love. I might have to carry out lowly tasks once we reach our destination, but with my reading skills and whatever learning I have, I might be fortunate in securing a post as children's nursemaid or even governess one day.'

Bob shrugged.

'Anyone who takes you for a horse thief must be an idiot. But I'm afraid you'll still set foot on Australian soil as a convict. I don't know how you'll fare — we don't know how any of us will, but if the captain thinks this reading lark's of use to you, then so be it.'

'Thank you. I'll still be with you for the rest of the day.'

'And the children usually sleep for some of the afternoon.' Mary nodded at Tabitha. 'It's a good idea and shows you've impressed the captain.'

'Thank you, Mary. The way he put all of us together has impressed me, too. I believe he's a good man.'

Tabitha felt the baby she cradled in her arms begin to stir. Looking down at his small countenance and seeing him pucker his lips as if seeking nourishment, she wondered if she would ever become a mother one day. Mary took her little one from Tabitha and began to feed him.

Tabitha turned to Bob.

'I'll take the other two up on deck if I'm allowed.'

'Mrs Gibbs is patrolling just now and she's usually all right about taking the children for a walk.'

'She's already told me she has two of her own, both boys working on the land. I think she took to a seagoing life after she was widowed. It must be strange, going backwards and forwards over the ocean.'

'Being a chaperone means she has no worries over rent or putting bread in her mouth. She could do very much worse.' Bob looked pensive.

'I apologise if I seemed uncaring at first but I'm aware of how men can behave, especially when they have power like Captain Learman.'

Tabitha looked at her boots.

'I appreciate your concern, Bob, but I know he's a good man.'

'Indeed. And I understand you must take any chance you can get to help you once we're in the new world.'

'Come, children. Time to take a look at the sea. I wonder what mood it's in today.' Tabitha took each child by the hand and turned to Bob. 'We'll see what words we can learn. What colours we might see in the sky and in the ocean. Already we've seen flying fish — such a pretty blue and silver! One day we might have sight of a whale.'

'Thank you for being so kind to my children.' Bob nodded to her.

She set off between the hammocks, a child either side.

* * *

Later, Tabitha made her way up from the prisoner deck after telling Mrs Gibbs where she was heading. The woman looked incredulous at first but waved her on just as Tabitha was wishing Captain Learman had issued her with a pass authorising her to quit her quarters. She felt excited at the thought of spending time with a book and wondered where she would sit. Any old corner would do.

When she arrived, she learned the captain was elsewhere, but a stern-looking officer heard her timid request and ushered her into the cabin.

'My orders are to show you this bookcase.'

The officer led her across the room and Tabitha couldn't help her eyes widening as she saw three shelves of assorted volumes, some bound with gold, others much plainer and some looking as though their pages had been turned countless times. Maybe by the boy destined to sail the high seas? Tabitha dropped to her knees and sucked in her breath. Where to begin?

She knew some of Wordsworth's poems and her mother had admired William Blake. She could start with one of these collections, she supposed. Yet, glancing back at the shelves, one particular book stood out. She reached carefully for it, sliding it from its place and balancing it on the palm of her left hand.

Puzzled to see its title was 'Charlotte Temple', also to find its author was a woman, she opened it. Tabitha was sitting on the floor, back against the wall, engrossed in her reading when Captain Learman arrived.

At once she scrambled to her feet, bobbing in his direction, and feeling herself blush, despite having permission to visit his cabin.

'Good day to you, Tabitha. Why are you not sitting in comfort?'

'I was quite comfortable, sir, in the corner; nor do I want to be a nuisance and get in anyone's way.'

'I believe it is I who am in your way. Please do continue with your reading while I sit at my desk. You may remain in your corner if you wish, but I should feel more comfortable if you were to sit in the big chair beside the bookshelves.'

He inclined his head and walked across the room.

Tabitha, still clutching the book, scuttled over to the big chair and sat down. Sitting bolt upright, her feet together, she returned to the story, losing herself once more in the world of a young woman who'd fallen in love with a British lieutenant.

As these fictional events unfolded, Tabitha's throat suddenly constricted as she found she was putting herself in the place of the heroine. But that was a ridiculous thing to do. Any self-respecting British lieutenant would never lower himself by falling in love with a convict! Calming herself with a deep breath, she continued reading until a knock came on the door.

'That will be tea,' Jacob said. 'Enter!'

Tabitha was about to close her book when she realised she had nothing with which to mark her place. Noticing her dilemma, Jacob rose and walked across to offer her a leather bookmark.

'Will you not miss this, sir?'

'I have another. You should mark your place and put the book back on the shelf. It's not one I immediately recognise.'

Tabitha marked her place and got to her feet.

'It's a lively book, sir. I meant to read poetry but I couldn't resist this story, especially as it's written by a female author.'

Jacob frowned and held out his hand.

'Please may I look? I can't think what this can be.'

Tabitha almost gasped when she felt his fingers brush her own as she handed over the book but his attention was on its title.

'I think I know where this came from,' he said. 'When my brother's wife packed a parcel of books for me, this one either got into the pile in error, or she's decided to influence my taste in reading. In case this was a genuine mistake, I'd better mention it when next writing to my brother.'

He gestured towards his desk.

'I'll pour you a cup of tea. Maybe

you'll tell me what poetry you enjoy and who first introduced you to it.'

Unbeknown to either of them, the cabin boy who'd brought in the tea, crouched, smirking, outside the door, one large ear pressed to the keyhole.

Distant Dream

Next day, before the evening meal, Jacob received a visit from the ship's padre.

The Reverend Percy Surridge, a man of around Jacob's age, accepted the captain's invitation to sit opposite him.

'May I offer you a glass of Madeira wine, Percy?'

The clergyman hesitated.

'Only if you're partaking, Captain.'

Jacob nodded and stood up.

'I'll be turning in early tonight as the ship's due to dock first thing in the morning.' He filled two glasses and handed one to the padre.

'Thank you, Jacob. I'm sorry I find it necessary to visit you on such a delicate matter, but I daren't shirk my responsibility.' He lifted his glass towards the captain.

Jacob raised his eyebrows.

'This sounds serious. Please tell me

what it's all about.'

'It's probably idle gossip, but I think you should hear it.' Swiftly Percy explained what he'd heard about the captain entertaining a young woman in his cabin.

Jacob sat back, frowning.

'Put like that, it does sound rather scandalous, but I trust you know me well enough to understand this is merely a friendly gesture. Tabitha Westwood has been the victim of a misunderstanding.'

The clergyman nodded.

'Unfortunately, it seems some members of your crew look upon your kind gesture as something much more fascinating. I intend doing my utmost to crush any rumours I hear in future, but it's a pity the young woman cannot read in privacy somewhere other than the captain's cabin.'

Jacob turned his glass around, watching the wine swirl before he drank.

'It seems I haven't thought this matter through, but you've given me an idea. If you'll allow, I'd like to seek your help.'

'I'll do my best to accommodate you.' Percy Surridge hesitated. 'You appear to feel strongly about this particular convict.' Seeing the captain open his mouth as if to protest, he sat back and waited.

'I admit to having a personal interest in her plight. I feel indignant on her behalf that some so-called horse trader should take such advantage.' In his turn, he hesitated.

'Your face tells me you doubt the truth of this. Please let me relate some of the information she gave me when I selected her to help Bob Lennox and his family through the voyage.' Quickly, he explained how Tabitha had set out, disguised as a boy, to avoid marrying the man her grandmother chose for her and how this led to her imprisonment.

'Now, please do me the favour of interviewing Tabitha, then see what you think.'

The clergyman drained his glass.

'I'll do that with pleasure. Perhaps it would be best if I come to your quarters tomorrow. I don't doubt your judgement but it would be helpful if I arrived at the same conclusion. And as your decision to allow her access to your day cabin seems to be creating comment, what if I were to chaperone this young woman while she reads?'

'You'd do that for me? Every afternoon, save Saturday and Sunday?'

'Of course. I always spend time in the afternoons, reading and meditating, so I see no problem making use of your accommodation rather than my own.'

* * *

Tabitha was taken aback the following afternoon when she arrived at the captain's quarters. As the ship had docked, its crew was involved with taking on board water and victuals to see everyone through the next stage of the voyage. But both the captain and the ship's padre were waiting when she knocked on the door. Upon being invited to enter, she hesitated on the threshold, curtseying as usual.

'Please come in, Tabitha. There's no need to look so worried. Our padre has kindly offered to remain here with you during your reading time.' Jacob looked across at Percy Surridge, who nodded at her.

'Tabitha, please be aware this arrangement is made so your reputation is protected and, of course, should you have questions arising because of what you're reading, our padre will be on hand to offer guidance.'

Tabitha bit her lip. What if the padre disapproved of the novel she'd chosen to read? Still, she murmured her thanks.

The captain gave her a low stool to sit on and the padre was offered the big chair. Tabitha's hand hovered beside a volume of Wordsworth's poetry but she longed to continue with the novel already begun, so selected it and settled herself.

The two gentlemen held a conversation in low voices for several minutes, but after the rowdiness of the prison decks, this presented no problem for Tabitha. Lost in a make-believe world, she didn't even notice the captain leaving.

After a while, the padre called to her and so engrossed was she, his sudden request startled her. She placed the bookmark between the pages, put down her book and walked across to his chair, standing, hands clasped before her.

'My child, I'm given to believe you have the ability to become a valued helper, maybe a nursemaid or even governess to a family. Captain Learman thinks highly of your abilities and Mr Lennox and his wife much appreciate your assistance.'

'Thank you, sir.' She'd no idea how she should address him but he looked steadily back at her. 'I'm indebted to the captain for instructing me to spend the voyage helping the Lennox family.'

'You've impressed him. What concerns me, my child, is the impetuous manner in which you appear to have left a good home.'

Tabitha felt her throat dry. Surely the padre didn't have the power to send her back on the next available ship? She gulped.

'I ... I couldn't bear the thought of being bound in matrimony to a man so much older than me.' She daren't mention his plumpness but hurried on. 'He was a man of the cloth — a widower who ...'

'Go on,' the padre said gently.

'My grandmother told me he was anxious to wed me and begin a family, sir. I felt unable to go through ...'

'It's all right, Tabitha. I understand your predicament, but couldn't you have made your views clear to your grandmother?'

'She is someone who expects to be obeyed. I didn't dare argue and I couldn't see any other way out than running away.'

Tabitha saw the clergyman frown.

'You could have met with even graver danger, despite your disguise. But even though your life is following an unexpected direction, you've encountered friendliness from Captain Learman.

'We still have many weeks left before we arrive in Victoria and your conduct throughout the voyage will be noted. I know you won't let either the captain or me down.'

'I appreciate your trust in me, sir.'

He bent his head to his own reading matter but not before Tabitha detected a glint of sympathy in his eyes.

★ ★ ★

One afternoon when Tabitha knocked on the captain's door, she heard him respond, then entered quietly as usual.

'Sit down, please, Tabitha.' He gestured to the chair opposite his desk. 'I'm in the process of writing a letter which I trust will be delivered as soon as we reach our destination. But I require your thoughts first.'

She seated herself. Why on earth did he need to discuss something with her? She was far too lowly to warrant such a thing. But she remained patient while he scanned the words he'd written and signed his name at the bottom of the page. Only then did he sit back and meet her gaze.

For moments, Tabitha forgot where she was. Forgot who she was. Forgot her past. Even forgot about the book she hoped to finish before long. All she could think of was the man sitting opposite. She would miss him more than she could possibly say.

And her future would take place without him, except when he walked through her dreams. She blinked hard, trying to concentrate upon what he was saying.

'This isn't the first time I've assisted prisoners in my charge to make a new life for themselves. The town of Fairclough isn't far from where The Lady Gwendoline will dock tomorrow.' He smiled. 'You're wondering what I'll say next, aren't you?'

She nodded.

'Most of your fellow countrymen will be taken to special encampments where they'll be assigned work. Some of them will do well and be able one day to acquire a parcel of land. The area is fertile and though not prosperous, holds hope for those prepared to work hard and behave as good citizens should and must.'

'I understand, sir.' She still wondered why he was taking such pains to explain the situation. Was he trying to warn her how her peaceful life on board must lead to one much rougher? A shiver travelled the length of her spine. Jacob was looking down at what he'd written again.

'I want to reassure you about your future,' Jacob said suddenly. 'This letter I've written is to a doctor friend who lives in the town I mentioned. He has a young family with twin girls needing more time than his dear wife can give.

'Their previous governess left suddenly and Dr Collins reported this fact in his last letter. I hope I've found a solution to his problem and the answer to the next step in your future. What do you say?'

She was apprehensive about what lay ahead, also saddened at the thought of parting from Bob and Mary and their children. But this man was once again thinking of her and she mustn't disappoint.

'I've no qualifications to offer, sir. It's years since my mother gave me lessons on the guitar and taught me something of the French language. But I'm grateful to you for thinking of me. Maybe I could help with domestic matters and free the doctor's wife to spend more time educating her children?'

He looked at her for some moments before responding.

'Your suggestion proves your potential to make more of yourself. You think things out in a sensible manner.' He grinned. 'Though it's to be hoped, if you do join the doctor's household, you won't suddenly take off in some new direction.'

Tabitha gasped.

'I doubt your friends would try to marry me off, sir!' She hesitated, fearing she'd spoken out of turn. Because, strangely, Jacob's expression was regretful. And at that moment she felt the same pain at the thought of never seeing him again. Of never knowing the joy of becoming married to the man she loved.

For, now the voyage was almost over, she knew for certain where her heart lay. But, although she might dream of becoming the captain's bride, that dream could never become reality.

A Kindly Welcome

Bright sunlight burning through her shawl. Rough, dry ground beneath her feet. Already Tabitha felt the searing heat prickling her neck, sending beads of moisture trickling down her back.

She was finally on dry land and it felt strange, walking on ground that didn't shift and sway. Her fellow-passengers all looked as she felt. Bewildered. Apprehensive. Unkempt. No wonder the small girl she'd grown to love over the last difficult months, clung to her hand so tightly. She was to accompany the Lennox family to the encampment nearby then wait to be collected.

All Tabitha's worldly goods were contained in the faded carpet bag Jacob had returned to her. Although she knew she should count her blessings over joining Dr Collins's household, her excitement was dampened by having to part from

Jacob Learman and before long, she'd say goodbye to people with whom she'd spent the last months.

Ahead of her trudged men, women and children. They seemed defeated before they even began this new life everyone spoke about. She wondered about Jenny, her friend from London. Where would she be sent? Might their paths cross again?

Word was being passed down the prisoner procession. Their temporary quarters were visible to those people at the front. Tabitha had been instructed to wait near the entrance. Who would collect her? What if the doctor changed his mind? Tabitha's heartbeat quickened at the thought of what might happen to her. Jacob was no longer her protector.

Someone was calling her name. She turned her head and to her delight, saw Jenny hurrying to catch her up.

'I'm glad to see you,' Tabitha said. 'At least we both survived the voyage.' At once she regretted making that remark. Her voyage had been a very different one from Jenny's.

Her friend almost stumbled and Tabitha grabbed her arm to steady her.

'Anyone'd think I was still onboard ship!' Jenny grinned. 'I've decided I'm going to work like there ain't no tomorrow and hope to find a farmer or someone like that to marry me!'

'My goodness! I hope you get your wish, Jenny.'

'What about you, Tabby?'

Tabitha knew better than to lie.

'I'm to join a doctor's household. Captain Learman decided I'd gained enough experience helping with the Lennox children to offer myself as a helper to another family.'

'Bless my soul! That's good to hear. But where does this other family live? Have you more travelling to do?'

'They live on the outskirts of town. Someone's supposed to be collecting me but I have to wait at the entrance to the encampment.'

'So, our paths may cross again. What's the name of this town?'

'Fairclough, Jenny. If only things were different! If only you too were going to a nice family and we could exchange addresses and... and keep in touch.'

At once she remembered her friend couldn't write. Tabitha felt saddened that she hadn't been able to begin teaching Jenny her letters because of the captain's decision to take her beneath his wing. She realised she'd been lucky but couldn't help wondering whether that luck would continue to hold.

* * *

Tabitha's spirits were low. She'd said goodbye to Jenny and wished her well. Now she stood, her bag at her feet, thanking her lucky stars for the early evening cool. This was spring in Australia but the changing seasons would have brought autumn to her homeland. She yawned, shuffling her feet and wondering what to do if she'd been forgotten.

She looked up, hearing a distinctive sound. A pony and trap were approaching, the pony's hooves kicking up reddish swirls. Whoever was driving must end up covered with that dust. She'd had very little to eat or drink that day and suddenly she yearned for a bed that remained still while she stretched out in it.

The driver called to the pony.

'Whoa, there, boy. Whoa, now…' He spotted Tabitha and called out. 'You for the doctor's house? Are you Miss Tabitha?'

'Yes, I'm Tabitha.'

'Then get up beside me. Throw your bag up first.'

Tabitha did as he said. She settled herself beside him and he clicked his tongue against his teeth and pulled on the reins. The pony set off again at a trot and Tabitha wondered why the man hadn't given the animal some rest.

As if he'd read her mind, the driver spoke.

'The house isn't far away.'

Tabitha frowned. What was that accent?

'Where are you from?' she asked. 'I'm

sorry, nobody told me the name of the person who'd be collecting me.'

He touched his cap.

'The name's Will Mackie. Born in Glasgow. Worked in the dockyard then got carried away by the promise of a job in London and ended up homeless. I stole to stay alive.'

'So, that's why you're over here?'

He shot her a curious glance.

'Aye. Beg pardon for asking, miss, but with you speaking so nicely and being a governess and all, how come you arrived on the convict ship?'

'It's a long story, Mr Mackie.'

'You can call me Will.'

'Thank you. And it would be good if you called me Tabitha.'

'Better not, lass. Unless you happen to call on me and the missus at home.'

'That sounds lovely. But to answer your question, I too was led down the garden path but I lived in Lancashire, not London.' She was about to admit she'd never before been employed as a governess but decided against it.

He whistled.

'You've come a long way too. Must've been hard on your family, seeing you carted off to Blackfriars?'

'I've hardly any family left, I'm afraid. How about you?' This man, she realised, was as easy to talk to as her father had been.

'Lost touch with my sisters and brother. Married a local girl ten years ago — daughter of the farmer I used to work for. Me and the wife have three nippers. My Nellie's a good seamstress. The doc's wife heard about her and she's Nellie's best customer now.

'I got my job with the family after their old employee retired. Nearly on his knees he was, poor fellow! Taught me a lot though. I'm Jack of all trades now.'

'Are the doctor and his wife good people to work for?'

'I should say so! Kind as a rainbow, the doctor is. His missus, too. Whoever put you forward for the governess job did you a big favour, miss.'

Tabitha relaxed. Though she doubted

Jacob Learman would have sent her to people he didn't have faith in.

She began taking notice of the surrounding countryside. There were fields either side of the road which wasn't much of a road but better than some she remembered from home. She wondered what kind of trees she could see. And were there kangaroos in this area — koala bears maybe? She had very little knowledge of Australia and never dreamed she might end up living here.

She turned to Will.

'I think the children had a nursemaid before me?'

'Indeed they did. She found herself a husband and left in a hurry.' His eyes twinkled as he glanced sideways at her. 'Reckon you'll find yourself snapped up too — sooner rather than later.'

'That I very much doubt, Will. Small children require a lot of attention and I need to make a success of this job. I'm fortunate to have been recommended and can't risk letting people down.'

'Sorry if I spoke out of turn, lass.'

'Ah, I didn't mean to snap at you. I'm only here because my grandmother had a mind to marry me off. But that's another story.'

'We're at the doctor's place now, anyway.' He pointed his whip. 'You can just see the roof above those eucalyptus trees. The house is only on one floor but there's plenty of room. The nursemaid's — pardon me, I mean the governess's — quarters are next to the children's rooms.'

Tabitha closed her eyes for moments. They felt gritty and no wonder. But the thought of sleeping in a proper bed with no-one else in the room to cough and snore and call out in the night... She reopened her eyes. Will was driving down a track, slowing the pony because of the rutted surface.

Moments later, she saw the house as the pony continued clip-clopping his way up the gentle slope. Will brought them to a halt and dropped the reins before jumping down.

'I'll give you a hand,' he called.

Tabitha had waited for this moment but still felt panic-stricken at the thought of yet another group of strangers judging her — other servants who might resent her presence, whether or not they were aware of her background. Will was waiting to help her. She stood up, reached for his hand and landed safely on the driveway.

'I'll get your bag and see you inside.'

She swallowed hard, ran her fingers through her dishevelled hair and waited while he rapped on the door. Moments later, a woman wearing a maid's uniform, opened it.

'This here's the new governess, Kitty.'

'I can see that, Mr Mackie.' The maid stood back. 'Come in, if you please. Mrs Collins will see you in the sitting-room. You can leave Miss Westwood's bag in the hall, Mr Mackie.'

Tabitha thought the maid sounded more formal than she'd expect, having been impressed with Will's friendliness. But she stood in silence, waiting to meet her new employer. What would this first encounter bring? How dreadful it would be if she recognised disappointment or even disgust in Mrs Collins's eyes...

The maid tapped on a nearby door.

'Come in,' Tabitha heard a voice call. Kitty stood in the doorway. 'Miss Westwood, ma'am.' She beckoned to Tabitha to enter.

Tabitha almost stumbled as she walked forward. The floor was polished wood, with colourful rag rugs here and there. There was a fireplace in which stood a piece of driftwood. Above the fireplace hung a portrait. Dressed in her dreary brown convict frock, she felt like a rag bag.

'You must be exhausted, you poor dear.'

Tabitha looked towards the speaker. Mrs Collins sat on an overstuffed couch in front of an open window. The lady of the house looked neat and clean and cool.

Tabitha looked up at the portrait again and realised who the subject was. Her skin was dusky and her eyes dark with well-defined brows and lashes. She wore her glossy black hair tied back from her oval face. Her pale pink muslin gown was immaculate.

Tabitha, awe-struck, wondered what her new employer would make of her and stammered out an apology for her dishevelled appearance.

Mrs Collins shook her head.

'I know something of the conditions in which you've travelled, my dear.' She eyed Tabitha's dress. 'I don't suppose you have something you can change into?'

'I'm afraid my only other garment is even shabbier than what I'm wearing, ma'am.'

'No matter. You shall wash and I'll find you something to wear from my wardrobe. We're about the same size and I don't think we need reminders of why you're here. But first, I suspect you need something to drink and eat.' She looked at the maid still standing in the doorway. 'Take Miss Westwood to the kitchen, Kitty, and look after her needs, please.'

'Yes, ma'am.'

Mrs Collins nodded to Tabitha.

'We'll speak later, my dear. My husband will be home then.'

'Yes, ma'am. And when will I meet my charges, please? Though I wouldn't want them to be frightened to see such a scarecrow!'

Her employer met her gaze and Tabitha feared her comment was out of place. But Mrs Collins's smile was kind.

'The children have been staying with my sister while we've been without a governess. They will be pleased to meet you, but this will happen in the morning, after their return. Your borrowed garments, though modest, will suffice until I can arrange to have dresses made for you.'

Tabitha bobbed a curtsey. The doctor's wife got to her feet and walked towards her.

Mrs Collins gently touched Tabitha's cheek with the fingers of one hand.

'Captain Learman explained to my husband how you came to be transported.

'Dr Collins and I are happy for you to live with us because we realise how unjust the law courts can be. However, you may find some people are suspicious of you — perhaps because they've listened to gossip. Tongues always wag when a newcomer arrives in Fairclough.

'The same applied to me after I met my husband and he brought me here as his wife. Hold your head high. Prove to everyone that Captain Learman's opinion of you is accurate, which I'm sure it is.'

Tabitha nodded.

'Thank you, ma'am,' she whispered and backed out of the room before the tears threatening to fall could do so.

Lost for Words

Where was she? Why could she hear a cock crowing when there were no hens aboard? Tabitha opened her eyes. She lay in a bed, not a bunk. There was no movement. No hullabaloo as people stumbled past. Realisation flooded her as she remembered her whereabouts.

Quickly she jumped from beneath the blankets and pattered across to the window, pulling open the shutters. Sunlight streamed in but she'd no idea of the time. She was about to get dressed when she heard the door at the end of the corridor open.

'So, you're up and about already? It's still early. When you come to the kitchen, you and me can break a crust together. There's fresh milk from the cow.'

Kitty retreated and Tabitha felt relieved, knowing she wasn't expected to join her employers so early in the day, especially as she was still in awe of the doctor.

She shut herself in her room again and poured water into a bowl so she could splash her face. She dressed quickly, decided the simple gingham dress fitted very well then dug into her bag, her fingers finding her mother's hairbrush. Using it soothed her spirits. Tabitha gave a little twirl before pushing her feet into her boots and leaving the room.

She found Kitty chopping vegetables.

'Can I help?' Tabitha asked. 'Are you the cook as well as the maid, Kitty? Goodness, you must be kept busy.'

The woman raised her eyebrows.

'You're friendlier than that one that used to be here. But I need no help, thank you. Sit yourself down. Cut yourself some bread and I'll be there before long.'

Tabitha was eyeing the food. After shipboard rations, the soup she'd eaten last night and the freshly baked loaf in front of her were manna from heaven. She cut herself a slice of bread, spread it with yellow butter and almost swooned with delight as Kitty placed a honey-comb upon the table.

'I've kept a boiled egg for you. If ever a body needed feeding up it's you!' Kitty put down the brown egg beside Tabitha's place. 'You're a lucky young woman to have survived that long journey.'

Seeing the curiosity in her eyes, Tabitha knew the maid must wonder what crime the new governess had committed. She nodded.

'I'm fortunate indeed. Some time I'll tell you my story, Kitty. Believe me, I'm no thief. Nor am I a woman of ill repute.'

'I never thought that for one minute, Miss Westwood.'

'Please can you call me Tabitha? At least while it's just you and me in the kitchen?'

Tabitha watched Kitty's expression change and knew she'd made a friend.

'All right. Tabitha it shall be. Now, eat up and be ready for the mistress to speak to you about your duties. There's company arriving for luncheon today so I'll be busier than usual.'

with delight as Katy placed a honey-
comb upon the table.

Jacob Learman awoke in his hotel room. For moments he wondered where he was. Of course, he was between ships once more. For several days he could forget his duties and enjoy the mild Australian spring.

When he eventually sailed back up the River Thames to Blackfriars, it would be to the bleakness of a British winter, though he doubted he'd make England before December. As always, it would depend upon prevailing winds and good fortune.

Collecting his thoughts, he realised he must visit George and his family, possibly even stay with them now he'd made a formal proposal of marriage to his friend's sister-in-law.

She danced in his head again. But not Caroline. No, it was Tabitha he carried with him like a lucky gold charm. What kind of man was he? Why couldn't he realise he was due to sail back and claim his bride to be? His thoughts shouldn't dwell on the girl whose sparkling brown eyes and ridiculously creamy skin persisted on tantalising him.

Today he was to lunch with his friend, the good Doctor Collins, and his beautiful wife. Would he see Tabitha? It would surely be the last time before he sailed.

But the governess wouldn't be lunching with her employers and their guest. This was her first day of employment. She'd had no time to settle in and acquaint herself with her charges and the domestic routines.

He'd done his best to ease her path into this strange new world which was now her home. It was time to let go. But why should he feel so miserable? There could be no future for Tabitha Westwood and Jacob Learman. This thought caused a pang so sharp, he groaned aloud.

He closed his eyes, struggling to picture golden-haired Caroline. Well, if he found difficulty, that was understandable, wasn't it? They hadn't seen each other for many months. Whereas he and Tabitha had met almost every day of the voyage. He'd become used to her company. But that situation was no longer. Doubtless, when the time came, she'd find a suitable husband. Someone nearer to her age…

He got out of bed. The hotel wasn't far from *The Lady Gwendoline*'s berth. He smoothed his beard and decided to visit a barber before his luncheon appointment. Dr Collins's note awaiting him last night stated he'd be sending someone to collect him from the hotel at noon. It would be good to see his friends again. Jacob told himself he'd been too long at sea, giving too much of his thinking time to unsuitable daydreams.

It was time to return to earth. Perhaps Flora Collins could advise him regarding a suitable present for his intended? Choosing a betrothal gift would surely convince him, as well as Caroline, of the sincerity of his intentions?

★ ★ ★

Her new charges stood, hand in hand and side by side before the fireplace when

Tabitha entered the parlour. Each twin wore a pale green cotton dress. Each little girl looked as though butter wouldn't melt in her mouth.

'Miss Westwood, may I introduce my daughters?'

'I'm Daisy and she's Edie!' They looked at Tabitha expectantly. Their mother caught Tabitha's eye. Tabitha knew she'd be safe and happy here. Her employer was smiling.

'Why don't you two show your governess the gardens before you start work? Is that all right, Miss Westwood?'

'I'd like that very much. I'm looking forward to seeing your spring flowers.'

The rest of the morning passed quietly. Tabitha felt pleased about her first meeting with her charges and ate lunch with them before reading a story from a book in the nursery bookcase.

Their mother had given strict instructions that the children were to rest in the early afternoon and, sure enough, two pairs of eyelids were drooping by the time the story finished. Tabitha escorted them to their bedroom, making sure they were settled before returning to her own room.

Having requested permission to borrow a book from the bookcase in the hallway, she lay on her bed to read.

She must have dozed off, because on waking, she heard voices floating upwards from outside. Might this be the company Kitty had mentioned earlier?

Tiptoeing across, she peered cautiously out. Her heart appeared to leap in her chest, so surprised was she to see Captain Learman. But Jacob stood alone now, gazing at the garden. Where were his host and hostess? So near and yet so far ... dare she hurry down to speak to him?

* * *

Jacob had mixed feelings. He'd enjoyed a good lunch with his friends. He told them he'd proposed to Caroline and felt sure this was a wise decision. At that point, he thought Flora looked strangely at him, as if doubting his sincerity. But he'd pushed away the thought. His hostess had gone upstairs to rest, and while he was enjoying his coffee, the maid knocked on the door with an urgent message.

The doctor had left in a hurry, grabbing his medical bag after shaking hands with Jacob and assuring him Will Mackie would drive him back into town once he returned from the hospital trip.

Now, alone in the garden, listening to the song of a bird he couldn't identify, he longed to hurry indoors and ask the maid if he could speak to Miss Westwood. He was scolding himself for being a chump when he heard his name called and light footsteps approaching. Whirling around, he stood face to face with Tabitha. Without hesitation he reached for her right hand and cradled it between his. They stared at one another, lost for words.

She held his gaze.

'I … I saw you from my window and couldn't resist coming to say goodbye again. I … I hardly recognised you without your beard!'

He squeezed her hand but still clung to it.

'I didn't ask to see you, in case I disturbed Flora and the children. So, you think you'll be happy here?'

'Oh, yes, I do. Captain Learman, you've shown me such kindness. When I think of how I might have been treated, had you not found me this position ...'

'Hush, no need for dark thoughts. And I think you might call me Jacob now you're no longer under my care. What do you say?' He watched her face light up.

'Of course. Thank you, Jacob. How ... how much longer do you stay in Fairclough?'

He wanted to say not long enough.

'Several days, mostly spent supervising the loading of my next ship and spending time in the shipping company's offices.'

In a wild moment, he considered inviting her to take supper with him at the hotel next evening. But that would scandalise the doctor and his wife and might place Tabitha's position at risk. Common sense prevailed and he quashed any thoughts of asking permission to write to her. Reluctantly, he released her hand.

'I must go to the children,' she said. 'They'll be waking soon and I don't want them to disturb their mother. She's a very kind lady, Jacob. I do realise not everyone would allow a convict into their home, let alone permit her to tutor their children.'

'Flora knows your story, Tabitha. She agrees with me it's quite evident you should never have been transported.' He hesitated. Silently he thanked his lucky stars this young woman had been sent to his ship.

'Farewell, Tabitha. I wish you good health and happiness.' He couldn't bring himself to tell her, should their paths cross in future, he'd be a married man.

'Goodbye, Jacob. I wish the same for you.'

She stood on tiptoe and kissed his cheek, so swiftly, so lightly, he felt the touch of her soft lips far too fleetingly.

But before he could undo all his good intentions, she was fleeing from him. Returning to her new life, leaving him alone with his thoughts, while his fingers touched the freshly shaven cheek her lips had caressed.

A New Admirer

The months went by and Tabitha had her hands full with two lively children to supervise and their mother handing more and more responsibility over now she was with child. Tabitha didn't mind working hard. She'd grown fond of the children and their mother, and Dr Collins, after his initial reserve, was pleasant and appreciative so her working hours passed pleasantly.

Slowly she learned not to think of Jacob as the days went by. Christmas came and went and she realised one morning he was probably back in London.

Acknowledging such a man must surely be married or betrothed, she agreed to attend a dance being held at a nearby farm the following Saturday night. Kitty, the dark horse, or so Tabitha called her, confessed to having an admirer and was hoping for a marriage proposal.

'Benjamin Gingham lost his wife early last year,' she said. 'He's a decent man and though I'm happy here, I don't want to remain in this job till I pop my clogs, now do I? I know he sorely misses his helpmeet and I'm willing to work hard and hope to please him.'

Tabitha saw the reasoning in that. But she didn't expect to hear what came next.

'Mr Gingham has a son who works with him on the farm. His name's Archie and he's twenty. It's time you had a night out and Archie's keen to meet you. What d'you say?'

'Surely you and I can't both go out at the same time?'

'I'll speak to the mistress. She knows my younger sister who works in town and who'd keep an eye on the girls, so long as Mr Mackie can collect her and take her back.' Kitty winked at Tabitha. 'He has a liking for my peach pie. Says it's better than his wife's recipe but on no account is she to know!'

Tabitha chuckled.

'In that case, yes, I'd like to go to the dance but I don't know what I can wear.'

'Gracious me, one of your everyday frocks will do fine.' She bustled off, leaving Tabitha to prepare a light meal for the children. As she cut slices of peach pie, she wondered what Archie Gingham was like. But she wasn't seeking a husband.

After she settled the children into bed on the Saturday, Tabitha reported all was well to their mother before hurrying to her room to change into the pretty rosebud-sprigged muslin gown Flora insisted she borrowed. There was also a pair of lightweight shoes and an emerald green ribbon to tie back her hair. She picked up a white shawl she'd bought with some of her wages and arrived in the kitchen where she found Kitty waiting.

Tabitha gasped.

'My word, you look lovely, Kitty. I wouldn't be surprised to hear Mr Gingham proposes marriage to you tonight.'

'And you're a picture, Tabitha. That gown could've been made for you.' Kitty hurried to the back door and peered out. 'That's Mr Mackie coming up the drive. Soon as my sister's inside and settled, he'll take us to the dance.'

★ ★ ★

The farm wasn't far away and after a few minutes of rattling along country lanes in the twilight, Will Mackie pulled up alongside a big barn which he told Tabitha was a wool shed, empty at that time of year. He assured her he'd drive her and Kitty back later.

'But maybe your admirer will insist on driving you back, Kitty?' he teased.

'Do you know everything that happens in these parts, Will Mackie?' But Kitty was in a good mood, catching hold of Tabitha's hand and leading her into the woolshed.

Tabitha could hear the sort of lively music that made her want to tap her toes. Inside, most folk were standing around or seated in groups so she and Kitty found a quiet corner and watched

136

the dancers.

'Which one's Mr Gingham?' Tabitha asked.

'He's coming across now!'

Tabitha saw a bearded, powerfully built man, probably ten years older than Kitty. He nodded a greeting to her, took Kitty's hand and swept her away.

Tabitha wondered where Archie Gingham was. If he was that keen to meet her, why hadn't he come over with his father? She hoped she wasn't going to be left sitting down all night.

'Miss Westwood?' A slim young man, his hair jet black and curly, stood in front of her. 'Would you care to dance? I'm Archie Gingham.'

Tabitha nodded and smiled.

'Pleased to meet you.' She got to her feet and followed him on to the make-shift dance floor.

Archie took her in his arms and whirled her away so fast she had a job keeping up with him. They jigged around the floor until the musicians announced they were taking a rest and Archie took Tabitha by the hand and led her to a table where jugs of lemonade stood ready. She drank the cool liquid gratefully, looking round to see if she recognised anyone and almost spluttering when someone tapped her on the shoulder. She turned to find her friend Jenny grinning at her.

'I knew I'd meet you again some time, Tabby!' Jenny flung her arms round her. 'My, you look in the pink.'

'The food probably has something to do with it!' Tabitha gazed at Jenny. 'You look well, too. Where do you work?'

'I'm maid to an elderly couple. They're really kind to me and their house is in the middle of town. How are you getting on?'

'I'm happy with the doctor's family. The house isn't far from here and I rarely go into town so no wonder we've not met before.'

Tabitha was aware of Archie standing patiently by and moved to include him in the conversation.

'Jenny, this is Archie Gingham. His father owns this farm. And Archie, this is my friend, Jenny. We met on the voyage over.'

Tabitha startled herself by the way she hadn't tried to hide her background. Kitty must have told Archie's dad anyway and she still determined to walk tall, as Mrs Collins had advised.

'Pleased to meet you, I'm sure.'

Tabitha decided Jenny was bowled over. Archie was a fine-looking fellow but he'd taken Tabitha's hand back in his and though smiling politely, obviously wasn't interested in listening to the girls chattering.

She turned to him.

'Jenny and I haven't seen each other for months, Archie. Do you mind if we catch up for a few minutes?'

He shrugged.

'It's fine by me. But I don't want to lose you to one of the other fellers. If someone asks you to dance, would you mind telling 'em you're spoken for, Miss Tabitha?'

'My goodness … um, yes, all right then. We won't be long.'

Archie moved off.

'He ain't gone too far,' Jenny whispered. 'I reckon he's smitten all right. How long have you two been seeing each other?'

'We met for the first time this evening.'

Jenny laughed out loud.

'And already I can hear wedding bells ringing. Well done, girl!'

Tabitha's heart almost stopped beating, or so it felt. Her self-control and determination over the last months melted like butter pats left on a sunny window-sill. She knew for sure there was only one man she wanted to marry.

'That won't happen. I enjoy my work and I'm continuing to learn all the time so I keep ahead of the children. One day, I'd like to be qualified to teach in a proper school.'

Jenny stared at her.

'Tell me those rumours weren't true.'

'What rumours?'

'About you and the captain. Everyone knew you were sweet on him and he on you. Did he make advances?'

Tabitha's cheeks were burning and there was a drumming sound in her ears.

'Jenny, the captain was a true gentleman at all times. He was only ever interested in helping me improve my situation.'

'If that's what you believe, then so be it. I don't want to fall out wiv you, Tabby, but likely you wasn't the only girl on that ship wrongly convicted of a crime.

'Yet he picked you out, didn't he? I always stood up for you when the harpies gossiped but I reckon you still hold a torch for the captain and that's why you're not interested in Archie.'

'Jenny, it's unlikely Captain Learman's not married! It's a fat lot of good me mooning over someone else's husband, now isn't it?'

'I s'pose. Anyhow, if you ask me, that Archie's a much better bet. Not much older than us, I reckon, and pretty enough to eat!'

'What will I do with you? But it's good to see you again. You and I went through such a lot together.'

'You oughter write it all down one day. Do you send letters to your family?'

'You mean my grandmother?'

'Oh, sorry, Tabby, I'd forgot your folks is dead.'

'It's all right. I wrote to Grandma, giving my new address but she's probably still too furious to answer my letter. Hey, the music's starting again and there's a young man staring at you. I think he's coming to ask you to dance.'

Jenny turned away to face her new partner and at once Archie was at Tabitha's side.

'Please may I have the pleasure, Miss Tabitha?'

She hoped he wouldn't claim her for every dance, but she'd no intention of upsetting him. Already she was feeling much more at home in Victoria. And if it was her destiny to remain there, she must accept that.

Heading for Heartbreak?

Jacob had been stuck in port at Capetown for several days and when at last his ship sailed, he still hadn't heard from Caroline.

Now and then, Tabitha's face still appeared in his mind's eye, although he'd learned to prevent his thoughts from wandering too much. He was even considering seeking employment other than as a ship's captain, feeling, at times, strangely unsettled and wishing for a proper home and family of his own.

Obviously, that must wait until he'd placed an engagement ring upon Caroline's finger and they could discuss their nuptials and their future together. They hadn't seen one another for about eight months and if she'd written to him during that time, her letter must have gone astray.

He worried she might never have

received his proposal and was already promised to another.

At last the day came when Jacob guided his ship safely back to Blackfriars Bridge. He sent a messenger boy to his friend George's house, stating his intention to stay at his brother's residence that night and would call upon George or indeed his wife or sister-in-law, should George be away at sea. Jacob needed, of course, to wait until fully relieved of his responsibilities.

He received no reply from George or his wife and it was around four o'clock next day that Jacob took a horse-drawn carriage from his brother's house to Knightsbridge. Jacob passed the journey deep in thought as to what lay ahead. Not for the first time, it occurred to him Caroline might be out of town.

Jacob alighted from the carriage outside George's house, paid off the driver and took the flight of shallow stone steps two at a time. The imposing brass knocker gleamed as brightly as usual and within moments someone opened the door. To his amazement, Caroline stood there, fresh and pretty in her blue velvet gown and fur tippet. Temporarily robbed of speech, he made a swift bow and reached for her hand, to land a kiss on the back of it.

'This is a surprise! Please, come in, Jacob. I'm pleased to see you again, though I'm afraid George and my sister have taken the children to visit their grandparents.' Caroline stood back to let him enter.

'I hope you're not alone in the house, Caroline. Are there no servants with you?' His mouth was dry, his heart beating too quickly, his thoughts in turmoil.

She led the way to the parlour.

'I'm on my own with two servants to look after everything. I happened to be gazing through the window when your carriage pulled up, so I took it upon myself to open the door. I'll ring for tea, Jacob. Do take a seat beside the fire.'

A maid arrived within moments and Caroline sat down opposite him, with a strangely wary look upon her face, he thought.

'My dear,' he began, 'I trust you received my marriage proposal.' She gasped, but he persevered. 'I'm sad to say I've heard nothing from you in return, so can only assume your response was lost in the mail. Dare I ask whether you received my proposal favourably?'

She was looking at him with amazement.

'But I answered your letter months ago. Are you saying you never received it?'

'Well, it would seem so.' He got up and went over to her, kneeling and reaching for her hands to clasp them between his own. 'I'm very sorry to hear this but let me make amends now we're together again. Caroline, will you do me the honour of becoming my wife?'

There! He'd said the words. But why did he feel no rush of joy? Nor, apparently did Caroline. Her expression spoke volumes.

He'd been about to reach for the beaten silver bracelet he carried in his pocket, but instinct told him otherwise.

'Jacob, I can't accept your proposal, because ... because I'm promised to another.'

Slowly he released her hands and got to his feet again.

'You're engaged to be married to someone else?'

She nodded.

'I'm so sorry. After your letter arrived, I took some time to reply because I had by then met another young man at a party and he'd begun calling.'

Jacob's head swam.

'So, you wrote a letter, turning me down, and all these months, I've been wondering whether we were engaged or not?'

She gave him an anguished look as the tea tray was brought in. They sat in silence while cups were filled and macaroons offered and the maid left them alone again.

'I was of course flattered by your marriage proposal, Jacob, but because Thomas had entered my life, I didn't think it fair to … to…'

'To keep me dangling on the end of a string?'

'Exactly! But, poor dear Jacob, it seems that's exactly what has happened and through no fault of my own, I assure you. I took pains to compose a letter I thought explained my decision honestly.' She was looking at him with a woebegone expression.

'Drink your tea,' he said gently, picking up his cup though his thoughts were whirling.

She raised her teacup to her mouth and for the first time he noticed she wore a thin gold ring on the third finger of her left hand. He thought the gemstone was a sapphire.

How had he not noticed it earlier? Probably because he'd believed he and Caroline were to become formally betrothed. Yet, here he was, still a free man, though numb with shock.

'I hope we can remain friends, Jacob. One day I hope you'll find happiness and perhaps settle down in London?'

'Who knows?' He gave a wry smile. 'Does your future husband work in the city?'

'He does.' She met Jacob's gaze. 'I've seen my sister spend too many lonely hours with George away at sea. To be honest, I'm relieved not to be placed in that position.'

At that moment, he realised how badly he'd misread Caroline's situation, having imagined her sitting at home, waiting for him to make advances.

Yet he didn't feel heartbroken as he knew he ought. She was pretty. She still smelled of flowers. But she'd never made him feel as he felt when he thought of the brown-eyed girl with the glorious copper tresses. He refused an invitation to dinner and to meet Thomas, giving the excuse that his brother and sister-in-law would be expecting him.

He hailed a cab and was driven back to his brother's house where he dined with his hosts, still dazed by the afternoon's revelations but deciding not to confide in anyone. He needed time to absorb this news and time to reflect upon his future.

He decided to leave London and take himself off to Brighton. He enjoyed Brighton in winter and planned to take long walks, read and think.

And when it was time to report to the shipping company once again, there was no question of handing in his notice and leaving his employment after his next two voyages.

Jacob's one thought was whether to renew his acquaintance with Tabitha Westwood. He knew what he wanted, but must possess himself in patience. After all, she, too, might have attracted the attention of some young man looking for a wife.

Not the Right Man

It was the morning after the dance and Kitty was teasing Tabitha mercilessly.

'You're a fast worker, I'll say that for you! Once Archie clapped eyes on you, I could tell he was hooked for life!'

Tabitha knew she was blushing like a beetroot.

'Goodness, Kitty, just because I didn't dance with anyone else ...'

'And why was that?' Kitty was stirring a pot of porridge.

'Because Archie didn't leave my side for long enough and I don't suppose anyone else wanted to dance with me anyway.'

The older woman chuckled.

'Maybe they were all afraid Archie would see them off. Are you glad you went?'

'Yes, I wouldn't have met Jenny again if I hadn't.'

'Hmm … I should watch out for that wench if I were you. I saw her making eyes at Archie whilst she was dancing with someone else. Brazen, if you ask me.'

'Maybe, but I'm not looking for a husband. I'm still only seventeen and there's so much I want to learn. Being married would mean saying goodbye to all that.'

Kitty shook her head.

'Who knows?'

'It's obvious that becoming a farmer's wife would mean lots of chores, probably lots of children, and no time for studying.' Horrified, she remembered Kitty was on the verge of exactly such a fate!

'I'm sorry, Kitty. It's just that I've been given a second chance and I want to make the most of it. If marriage happens, I'd prefer it not to be too soon.'

'Well, that's told me, then!' Kitty began ladling out porridge.

'Shall I take those through?' Tabitha asked.

'That'd be kind. Where are the children?'

'With their mother. She's resting in bed and reading to them. I'll tell her their breakfast's ready.'

'She's fond of you, Tabitha. People take to you, don't they?'

'Not everyone does! Especially my grandma.' Tabitha had told Kitty about her past.

Kitty shrugged.

'More fool her. She'll probably regret what she tried to do with you. But do you ever wish you'd stayed put?'

Tabitha paused on her way out.

'I regret ending up in jail, but being transported meant I met people I became fond of. Also, I believe I have more chance of leading a full life here than I'd have had in England.' She still shuddered when she thought what her life might be now, had she not escaped.

The rest of the morning passed speedily, allowing no time for her to ponder Kitty's remarks. Archie was a handsome fellow but she thought it highly unlikely their paths would cross.

Nor would she make a suitable wife

for him — or anyone else — while Jacob still haunted her thoughts and dreams. She knew she was being ridiculous. She might be considered a suitable wife for Archie, but as for marrying a man of Jacob's calibre ... that only happened in fairy tales, didn't it?

★ ★ ★

Alone in his cabin, Jacob took out Tabitha's letter as if it was a box of sweetmeats waiting to be relished. She wrote a good hand, with excellent spelling and grammar. He'd made the right decision in recommending her to the doctor and knowing she was happy and in gainful employment meant a lot.

He'd also made another decision since Caroline's announcement. The postal service had failed him, but he'd been released from a life he realised would have been wrong for him and for her, too. He felt ashamed of his presumptuous thoughts and wished her happiness for the future.

As for his future? He'd had ample time to think while walking on Brighton's pebbly beach and strolling through lanes and byways. There was a project so dear to his heart, he could hardly bear to contemplate it for fear he was again thinking ahead without being certain his suggestion would be welcome.

He needed to purchase a suitable property, one where he could write and study and start a small school. The population in Victoria was growing and families would be looking to educate their children to help them on in life.

His decision made, he longed to share his thoughts with Tabitha. He didn't intend trying to steal her away from her current position. That wouldn't be fair, especially as his friends had housed her and entrusted their children to her care, on his recommendation.

No, the months would pass and it would take time to arrange everything to his satisfaction. Jacob intended to look at possible houses while in Fairclough this time, also to enquire whether he'd find it easy to rent a house when he returned after his last voyage, in case it wasn't possible to buy or build the right property in time.

He smiled as he thought how, after ensuring Tabitha's feelings matched his, he'd ask her to hear his plan and consider whether, one day, she would become his wife and work beside him in their new school.

He hoped Edward and Flora's children would become the first pupils, but he knew much depended upon Tabitha and, until he spoke to her, he daren't be too cock-a-hoop. Losing Caroline to another was what he deserved. Losing Tabitha, he knew now, would be a dreadful blow. But even if she turned him down, he resolved still to make a new life for himself in Australia.

* * *

The following Sunday afternoon, Archie's father arrived at the back door, asking to see Kitty. Tabitha answered his knock as

156

Kitty was in her room. Both she and Tabitha were allocated small but comfortable bedrooms and both appreciated their good fortune.

'Kitty? You have a visitor.' Tabitha waited.

Kitty poked her head around the door. 'Is it my sister?'

'Not your sister. This is a gentleman caller.' To Tabitha's delight, Kitty could still blush. 'Where is he?'

'Waiting at the back door. Looks like he wants to take you for a drive so you'd better look sharp.'

'Two minutes,' Kitty hissed.

Tabitha went back to report. Mr Gingham thanked her politely. She didn't like to walk away and wasn't sure if it was her place to invite him in. So, she asked after his family.

'All in good health, Miss Westwood. And my Archie asks to be remembered. He mentioned you specially, should I bump into you.'

'Please give him my best wishes, Mr Gingham.'

She hoped this innocent remark wouldn't turn into something more flirtatious but luckily Kitty appeared and Mr Gingham swept her off in his pony and trap.

Tabitha clapped her hands when Kitty confided in her later that she'd consented to become the second Mrs Gingham. But she felt concerned as to who might take over Kitty's position in the doctor's house. It was a relief when Kitty drew her aside later.

'I need to talk to you, Tabitha.'

'You look happy about it, whatever it is.'

'I hope everyone will be happy soon. I'm to leave my job two weeks from now and marry from this house before moving into the farmhouse.'

'So soon?' But Tabitha realised there was nothing to keep the lovebirds apart.

'It'd be very satisfactory to leave, knowing my replacement was already known to those left behind.'

'What are you trying to say? Don't keep me in suspense!' Tabitha felt puzzled.

'I wish to recommend my sister. You've met Muriel a few times, of course. She's not especially happy where she is and I feel sure she's ideal for the job.'

Tabitha nodded.

'I agree.'

'Now, I must get the potatoes peeled and the meat roasting,' Kitty said. By the way, when do you plan to see my future stepson again?'

'I have no such plan.' Kitty knew her cheeks gave her away. Archie had asked if he might drive her to the beach on the next Sunday she was free. She'd told him she needed time to herself — to mend garments and write letters.

He'd looked so disappointed, so crestfallen, Tabitha almost relented. But she daren't raise his hopes. He was a kind, considerate young man and would make someone a fine husband. But while she knew how foolish her hopes were, she felt it would be wrong to marry a man whose love she couldn't return.

True Feelings

Jacob stood on the quayside, enjoying the cool evening air. All his passengers had disembarked and items from the hold were being offloaded. With his duties completed, he'd be free to go to his hotel, looking forward to a meal and a stroll before turning in. Next day, he'd have a note sent to the doctor and perhaps an invitation to luncheon or supper would be forthcoming. It would be helpful to discuss his plans with his old friend.

He wondered how Tabitha was enjoying her new life. It would please him immensely to know she was content. But how would she receive his declaration?

'Captain Learman?'

Jacob swung round to face the speaker.

'Compliments of Dr Collins, Captain. He sent me to enquire whether you'd care to be his guest while you're between voyages. Make a change from the hotel, d'you see?'

'That's very considerate of the doctor. I remember you now — you're Mr Mackie, aren't you?'

'You must meet a lot of people, Captain. Yes, I'm Will and very pleased to drive you back, soon as you say the word.'

Jacob thought.

'Could you make my apologies to the hotelier, Will?'

'Pleased to, sir.'

'If you could tell him I'll be in tomorrow to settle up for any inconvenience caused? And I'll meet you here in about an hour.'

Will touched his cap and set off. Jacob walked the length of the quay and back, his experienced eye checking the vessel, the condition of her freight now unloaded and the behaviour of his crew. They would be sleeping on board, under the eagle eye of his officers.

As soon as he could, he climbed up beside Will Mackie. As they headed into the countryside, Jacob wondered if he'd see Tabitha that evening. Probably not.

Jacob reminded himself of one very important fact. He was a deal older than she was. Maybe she regarded him with affection — he hoped so — but it might only be as a mentor, an older brother or even an uncle with her best interests at heart.

Soon they were following the stony track towards the house and as Will brought the trap to a halt, Edward appeared at the top of the front steps then hurried down them.

'My dear Jacob, come in.'

Jacob grasped his friend's hand.

'I'm grateful for your kind hospitality. The hotel's clean and tidy but it's good to be with friends.'

'Excellent. My wife sends her apologies and she'll see you in the morning. We're expecting another child and Flora tires more easily these days.'

'My congratulations! I must say I envy you, old friend. I often wonder whether God might grant me a son or daughter, one day.'

Edward shot him a quizzical look.

'Your seafaring makes it difficult for you to find the right woman. But your letter tells me you're contemplating settling here! I'm intrigued, and delighted, of course. Come, let me pour you some wine. Kitty has made one of her beef pies. I'm sorry to say she's to leave us soon, but we're to gain the services of her sister.'

'Why is Kitty leaving?'

'She's marrying a farmer whose land adjoins mine. He's a widower and a good man.' Edward poured wine into two tankards. As they settled themselves, Jacob longed to ask after Tabitha but waited for Edward to mention her. Annoyingly, his old friend seemed disposed not to.

'I hope everything works out well for everyone concerned,' Jacob said. 'If my plans go as I hope, I'll have need of a housekeeper once I settle into my new life.'

'But that'll take some while to happen, I imagine? It's one of the reasons I offered you hospitality — so we could discuss the matter more easily.'

Jacob put down his wine.

'You look very serious. Do you disapprove?'

'Good heavens, no, Jacob. Far from me to tell a man his own business, even if I disapproved. I do wonder though, whether you'll miss London society.'

Jacob stifled a chuckle.

'I think not.'

'In addition,' Edward continued, 'I'm hard put to think how you'll find yourself a wife in this area. You'd do better in Melbourne, I believe. The daughter of a rich industrialist would be delighted to become the bride of a man such as you.'

'You flatter me, but the life I long for wouldn't appeal to most young women.'

Edward nodded.

'This is what intrigues me. What exactly do you have in mind? Prospecting? Import and export? The world is opening up for traders.'

'Indeed.' Jacob leaned forward, hands on his knees. 'But I'm contemplating a scholarly life. I yearn to teach, help children learn their letters so they may write their names, draft a letter and read documents as well as the stories which have entranced me since my boyhood. I want to write my own book one day. I have a particular story in mind but that's a very personal dream. Forgive me if I say no more.'

'I'm surprised you wish to become a teacher.'

'You don't approve?'

'It's not that. There is, I'm sure, a growing thirst for knowledge. The young woman you sent us is helping our children gain in knowledge every day. I'm aware Tabitha reads and continues her learning, always remaining one or two steps ahead of her pupils.

'I admire her for this, but there aren't many like her in these parts. As for founding a school, it's an admirable idea.'

Jacob rose and walked over to the window, to stand with his back against the glorious setting sun.

'I need a large enough house to contain a schoolroom, or maybe I can buy land to build upon.'

'I'd no idea you felt so strongly but I'll help in whatever ways I can.'

Should he confide his feelings about Tabitha? Jacob could imagine her working beside him, helping him achieve his dream.

'It would take,' Edward said, 'a very special kind of woman to share your vision.'

★ ★ ★

Tabitha carried her plate and cutlery out to the scullery. Kitty had already gone to bed, exhausted after a busy day. Supper for two was laid on the dining-room table and hearing the sounds of movement along the hallway, Tabitha knew the gentlemen were about to begin their meal. She resolved to leave them be until they were finished and back in the sitting-room when she'd clear away and wash up their dishes before retiring.

She yawned and put down her mending. The lamp was lit and her eyes were tired. She could hear the diners returning to the parlour. Tabitha had been trying not to think about Jacob since the mistress told her the captain would arrive that evening. If she allowed herself the luxury of dreaming about him, what would be the point?

She completed her tasks and left the kitchen pin-neat ready for Kitty next morning. The gentlemen might remain talking for a while yet. Tabitha wiped her damp brow with her handkerchief. The kitchen felt stuffy. She needed to step outside and take some air before bed. Stepping from the house, she gazed up at the darkened sky, stars glistening like crystals scattered upon soft, black velvet. A full moon painted the garden with silvery light.

'Tabitha? I hope I didn't startle you. It's Jacob.'

To hear his voice after all this time sent shivers of delight down her spine. Slowly she turned to face the man walking towards her. She couldn't move. She daren't let herself do so for fear of running straight into his arms. For that was what she wanted to do more than anything else in the world.

He was close to her now. So close, she could reach out and touch him. But before she could utter a polite greeting, he stepped even closer, put his arms around her and held her as if he never wanted to let her go.

Tabitha relaxed in his arms, eyes closed so she could pretend the embrace was something much more intense than a friendly hug. As if in a dream, she allowed him to tip her chin upwards. Was this really happening? The moment Jacob's lips touched hers, softly and a little hesitantly at first, she knew what she so longed for was really happening. Their kiss deepened, making Tabitha wish it would last forever.

He stopped kissing her but still held her in his arms.

'I'm sorry, darling. I apologise for my lack of consideration in taking you by surprise, but now I'm here with you... well, the truth is, I've fallen in love with you. I think it happened not long after we met, but at that time I was under the illusion that I was an engaged man.' He hesitated. Still she remained silent.

He tipped her chin upwards once again, his expression tender.

'You're not running away from me, then? Like you did from the clergyman?'

'I would never run away from you, Jacob. But what are you saying? You've been at sea for months. I'm so pleased to see you, yet I fear you may be a little light-headed. What if the doctor should step outside?' Still she didn't — couldn't — leave the shelter of his arms.

'Edward has gone to his room. I looked for you in the kitchen before turning in, then decided I needed some fresh air and a chance to stargaze. When I saw you ... well, there's so much I want to say, my dear, but let us enjoy the night sky for a while.'

He hugged her closer. She fitted nicely against him. It felt so right to rest her head against his shoulder and if this was a dream, she'd enjoy it while she could.

'I'd better let you go,' he murmured

all too soon. 'I'll seek an opportunity to talk to you again, but am I allowed one more kiss, my sweet girl?'

She didn't answer. There was no need. And when their kiss ended, Jacob murmured tenderly.

'I love you, Tabitha.'

'And I you, Jacob.'

* * *

After such a startling event, Tabitha knew it was inevitable she'd spend much of that night tossing and turning. She lost track of how long she spent chasing slumber in vain.

Next morning, Tabitha's recollection of last night's events flooded her mind, making her wonder whether Jacob holding her in his arms and kissing her had been a dream after all. Did he really say he loved her? And had she really dared to reveal her true feelings after all this time?

Tabitha washed her face and dressed quickly. Leaving her room, she realised the house was still quiet, so she tip-toed down the corridor and opened the kitchen door.

'Kitty, this is your last day as a single woman,' Tabitha said.

The older woman beamed as she cut bread.

'Who'd have thought it, eh? Me about to become Mrs Gingham! Oh, Tabitha, whatever will I do if he should change his mind? Men can be fickle creatures, you know.'

For moments Tabitha wondered if Kitty suspected something and was issuing a warning, but she banished the thought.

'He won't do anything of the sort. You're just what Benjamin Gingham needs and you know it! Now, what shall I help you with before I wake the children?'

Tabitha was taking newly baked bread and a dish of butter to the breakfast table when she realised the two men were standing by the window, talking quietly.

They glanced at her and she gave

a quick bob, taking care not to meet Jacob's gaze. The bond, if that was the right word, newly formed between the captain and herself, was too precious to risk breaking by taking advantage of this delicate situation.

Tabitha was very aware of her social standing. She was still classed as a convict even though the drab brown dress was long gone, thanks to Flora Collins.

Jacob would understand her plight. Tabitha left the room. Now, more than ever, she was determined to follow the advice Flora gave her when she first arrived. She would hold her head high.

The Words She Longed to Hear

The twins were over-excited about Kitty's wedding. Edie and Daisy were usually well-behaved and Tabitha didn't have the heart to be too stern. To distract them, she suggested they each drew a picture of the flowers and trees growing around their house. While they were employed, Tabitha wrote out a list of words she thought they should be able to spell. Before long, the girls were eager to share their works of art and she was discussing their pictures when someone knocked on the door.

'Come in.' Tabitha looked up.

'Good morning.' Jacob smiled at them all. 'Forgive the interruption, Miss Westwood, but I wondered if your pupils might like to ask me questions about life at sea?'

Edie and Daisy seemed, for once, struck dumb.

'Why, thank you, Captain Learman,' Tabitha said.' That's a very kind offer. You girls have the chance to talk to a real live ship's captain. Shall I start you off?

'And please sit down, Captain,' she said. 'May I begin by asking you what it's like to have so many people under your command?'

Jacob settled himself.

'At first, very daunting. I'd served under some excellent officers so had good examples to learn from.'

'How old were you when you went to sea?' Daisy piped up.

'I was ten years old when I joined my first ship.'

'Were they kind to you?'

'They were, Daisy. The captain had sailed with my father long before I was born and he kept an eye on me.'

'So you followed in your father's footsteps?' Tabitha leaned forward.

Jacob met her gaze.

'Yes, I couldn't wait to leave home and see countries I'd only read about. I think my mother missed me, though.

She wrote me long letters.'

'Do you have to sleep in a hammock?' Edie asked shyly.

'Never. I slept in a cot as a youngster, but these days I'm fortunate to have something more substantial.'

Tabitha listened to her pupils growing in confidence as they talked to Jacob. He took everything they asked seriously, answering, she was sure, honestly. She was impressed not only with his knowledge, but with the way he held the girls' attention. Although she wondered why he should trouble himself to spend time doing this.

He asked whether he could hear each of the twins read and even Edie, the quieter one, seemed eager to show off her skills.

Tabitha was loving every moment. Jacob concentrated upon the twins, so she could look at him whenever he spoke. She also learned things and knew her geography lessons would be more interesting in future.

At last, Jacob turned to her.

'I've taken up enough of your lesson, Miss Westwood. Thank you for allowing me to join in, but I should spend time with my hostess now.' He rose, giving her a warm smile.

'We've enjoyed your visit, haven't we, girls? We'll take a break now. Time for a little run around in the garden while it's not too hot. You may leave your lesson books where they are and I'll come and find you very soon.'

Jacob waited while the twins left the room then closed the door.

'Tabitha, I'm so proud of you.' He walked towards her. 'I wanted to see you engage with your pupils and now I know my idea has borne fruit, far beyond what I imagined.

'Those children are fortunate to have you as their teacher. I like to think many more will follow in their footsteps.' He was at her side now. 'It is sweet torture, feeling as I do about you, my love, yet being unable to tell the world how I long to make you my wife.'

Tabitha closed her eyes as his arms

enveloped her. His kiss was as welcome and as delightful as last night's. The notion of becoming Mrs Jacob Learman, so often imagined in her dreams, seemed not so nonsensical now.

She still feared gossip, though — even scandal — if people should suspect her of being involved with a ship's captain. And what if Flora should walk in? She drew back a little, hating to see the hurt expression in Jacob's eyes.

'Oh, please, don't look like that, Jacob! My love for you began when I was far too young to know what love was. Now I'm in my nineteenth year and you seek me out ... it's almost too wonderful to bear. Yet, I'm so afraid Mrs Collins will suspect something.'

He nodded.

'You're right. But after months at sea, you, my lovely Tabitha, are like an oasis glimmering in the desert — so near and yet so far.'

She chuckled.

'You'll be writing poetry next, Jacob. What a beautiful thing to say.'

He took her hand in his and kissed the fingers.

'I need to speak to Edward, my old and trusted friend. I know I can confide in him. He defied convention to marry his beautiful wife instead of the rich girl from Melbourne his parents selected. I'll tell him the love I feel for you won't go away.

'The plans I have for my future have one flaw, which is that so far, you're not included. Tell me, Tabitha, when the time is right, will you do me the honour of becoming my wife?'

For moments, Tabitha felt as though the world had stopped turning. As though even the birds ceased to sing. As though her heart skipped a beat. Speechless, she stared at Jacob.

He smiled gently.

'Please don't be afraid, my sweet. I realise I can't ask your father for your hand in marriage, but if he were still alive, I would assure him of my eternal love and determination to look after his daughter to the very best of my ability.

Do you doubt my intentions? Or is it that you fear I'm too old for you?'

'Oh, Jacob! No, no, of course I don't think that. And how could I doubt your sincerity after all you've done for me? No, it is I who I doubt. For how can I possibly be the woman you deserve to make your bride? Me, with my humble background and criminal record!'

There! She'd confessed the thing she most loathed about herself.

'Seeing how you conduct yourself, I think your background's probably less humble than my own. And as for being a criminal — after your seven-year sentence ends, I intend to ensure that false pronouncement is struck from the records.'

Jacob was down on one knee, holding both her hands between his own.

'You're part of my dream for the future. There's no-one I'd rather spend the rest of my life with. And with you by my side, I know we can make a difference to the lives of children, whether our own or the pupils we teach. I want to settle in Australia.

'But wherever we might live, I offer you my love and devotion, Tabitha Westwood. Will you make me the happiest man on earth by consenting to be my wife?'

Doubts and fears disappeared. Knowing he shared her own dreams, more than ever she longed to become his wife.

'Yes, Jacob. I'll marry you and do my utmost to give you the happiness you deserve.'

An Abrupt Ending

Jacob realised his friends would be aston-
ished by the news. He was determined
to tell them of his marriage proposal and
Tabitha's acceptance, rather than expect
her to do so. He waited until the evening
meal when he, Edward and Flora, were
gathered round the dining table.

'I have something to tell you,' Jacob said
as they began on their vegetable soup.
'Something which will doubtless surprise
and possibly concern you. But I hope
you'll hear me out and accept my decision.

'You've both known me for some years
and you, Edward, for longer than I care
to remember!'

Edward raised his eyebrows.

'This is concerning the plan you
shared with me, Jacob? You know how
pleased we both are, knowing you want
to settle here.'

'I do, my friend. Can you recall something you said during our discussion? How you felt it would be difficult to find the right woman to share my life?'

'Yes, I still believe that's very important.'

Flora leaned forward, eyes sparkling.

'Jacob, does this mean you have good news from the young lady in London? You were hoping she'd look favourably upon your marriage proposal.'

'My apologies, Flora. I should have told you before. Caroline's letter, rejecting my proposal, never reached me. Stupidly, I didn't write again, imagining she'd reply when she was ready. It seems she was waiting to hear from me, but in the meantime met a young man who I gather swept her off her feet. She's probably married by now.'

'Goodness, you must be very disappointed.'

'Fate moves in strange ways. Caroline and I spent so little time together but still I presumed she and I would be suited as man and wife because her sister married a friend of mine who's also a captain with the shipping company.'

'But that's not all you have to say, is it?' Edward poured more wine.

'No. Over the time I've known her, I've become more and more fond of a certain young woman. My position enabled me to make life easier for her during the voyage she undertook from England to Australia last year.

'Furthermore, I was able to ensure she went to live with a fine family who I knew would treat her with the respect she deserved. I've been proved right. I realised she enjoyed my company but my own feelings, which I subdued while stubbornly believing I should look elsewhere for a wife, have now become such that I've proposed marriage to this young woman. I'm delighted to say she has accepted.'

Flora clapped her hands.

'Another wedding! How exciting!' She frowned. 'But I'm puzzled, Jacob. How have we not met your bride-to-be if she lives nearby?'

Edward was ahead of his wife.

'We have met her,' he said quietly. 'She's already here, living beneath our roof. Is that not so, Jacob?'

Flora looked from one to the other.

'But surely you can't mean...?'

Jacob reached across and took her hand.

'Yes, Flora, Tabitha is whom I love.'

Edward sighed. Flora burst into tears. Jacob feared the worst.

★ ★ ★

Much later that evening, when everyone else had gone to bed, the newly engaged couple spent a few minutes together in the kitchen.

'While the three of us were eating dinner, I broke the news of our engagement. Don't look so worried, darling girl, everything will work out as we hope.'

'It must have been a shock. I worry about Mrs Collins as she's in ... in a delicate condition.'

'Flora was very surprised,' Jacob admitted, 'but she was concerned over losing you, rather than disapproving of our engagement. That's a great compliment to you. It's not easy to find the right person to entrust with your children.'

'I must go to her in the morning and reassure her I've no intention of leaving until we marry.'

'Yes, much as I might want to whisk you off to a parson, I'll need to spend time in London after my voyage, then return as soon as possible. By that time, I hope to have purchased a suitable house. I'm going into town tomorrow to meet with one or two people Edward recommends.'

'What did he think about our betrothal? Knowing my fate after I ran away?' Tabitha knew he must see her anxiety.

'Hush.' Jacob drew her towards him and kissed the tip of her nose. 'He's delighted for us. If he'd felt uncertain about employing you, he wouldn't have let you stay, now would he?'

'I suppose not. If they only knew how I've dreamed about becoming your wife ...'

'I'll try to live up to those dreams, Miss Westwood. There will, no doubt, be trials and tribulations along the way, but I've no doubt whatsoever about marrying you.'

'Nor I you! But I must take my leave now. Tomorrow will be a busy day and I have my maid of honour duties to think about. Will you be attending the wedding?'

He shook his head.

'I wouldn't have expected an invitation, though Edward has suggested the two of us spend some time at the festivities. He and the family will attend the marriage ceremony but Flora needs plenty of rest.'

They parted with a kiss.

* * *

Kitty's sister was now in residence. Muriel was as kindly as her elder sister, and Tabitha felt sure she'd soon become part of the household. At breakfast time, she found the sisters already in the kitchen.

'Good morning! I trust the bride-to-be slept well?'

'Eventually. After I stopped worrying about the bridegroom changing his mind and Archie losing the ring and the parson falling sick and …'

'Stop!' Both Muriel and Tabitha called at once and soon all three were laughing together.

'You should enjoy every minute of today. After all, you're the most important person. The one everyone will be looking at,' Tabitha said.

'I don't know about that. Archie won't be looking at his new stepmother and that's a fact.'

Tabitha puckered up her face.

'I thought you two got on well. What do you mean?'

'I mean Archie will be looking at you, that's all. You know he has feelings for you.'

Tabitha felt herself go hot and cold.

'I thought I'd made it plain I wasn't interested in finding a husband.'

'You seem to be getting on very well

with Captain Learman.' Kitty was looking at her, head on one side, a faint smile
on her face.

'He's always been very kind to me. You
know I wouldn't be here if he hadn't put
a word in with the doctor and his wife.'

'I'm not trying to upset you, Tabitha. I
wouldn't do that for worlds. I don't want
to see you get hurt, that's all. Especially
when there's someone your own age
who'd make a good husband.'

Muriel was ladling porridge into three
bowls.

'Leave the poor girl be! Here, breakfast's ready. There's plenty to do today
so don't dawdle, you two.'

What could have been an awkward
moment was gone. But Tabitha couldn't
help wondering what prompted Kitty to
speak out like that. Surely Archie wasn't
still carrying a torch for her? She'd done
her best not to offer him any encourage-
ment.

As Muriel prophesied, there was
plenty to do and before long, Will Mackie
arrived, pony and trap ready to be loaded

with food and drink to transport to the woolshed.

* * *

'May I have the pleasure of this dance, Miss Tabitha?'

Archie was smiling down at her. He would think her very rude if she didn't dance with him, but she was watching out for Jacob, even though she'd reminded him not to ask her to dance, for fear this caused comment.

Everyone knew why Tabitha arrived in Australia. It was no secret. Yet, she realised the situation might alter, if people suspected the doctor's friend of taking an interest in her.

Archie was still waiting so she followed him on to the dance floor. This was a sedate waltz and as they progressed, Archie told her how pleased he was for his father and Kitty to have found happiness together.

'One day, when he decides it's time to take life more quietly,' Archie said, 'he'll have a new, smaller house built for him and Kitty. That'll leave plenty of space in the old one for me and whoever I marry.' He looked meaningfully at Tabitha who tried to think of the right thing to say.

'I imagine it'll be a while yet before that happens,' she said. 'He's not that old, surely?'

Archie laughed.

'No, he's not. But it's good of him to make it clear he has my future in mind, don't you think? And I expect he's looking forward to grandchildren.'

Stunned, Tabitha was trying to think of a reply when Archie spoke again.

'I do have someone in mind, but I haven't dared bring up the subject yet.'

She felt the arm encircling her waist tighten a little. He was holding her slightly closer. Over his shoulder she could see Dr Collins and Jacob entering the room. When would this dance end, for goodness' sake?

But the musicians kept playing and Tabitha, keeping sight of Jacob, saw him turn his head and notice her. At once his expression brightened and he smiled and locked gazes with her. But Archie twirled her round, changing direction so they were lost in the midst of a crowd of dancers.

Did he do that on purpose? She was probably getting nervous for nothing, but instead of enjoying the party, she now worried Jacob might consider her to be a flirt.

To her relief, when Archie escorted her back to her seat, she noticed her friend Jenny sitting nearby.

'Let's go and say hello,' Tabitha said. 'She's on her own over there and I'm sure she'd love it if you asked her to dance.'

Archie muttered something but did as he was told. Jenny got to her feet and hugged Tabitha as they reached her.

'I couldn't get time off to come to the wedding,' Jenny said. 'But Kitty sent me an invitation so I walked here ... but don't let me stop you two from dancing.'

'I expect Archie's pleased to have a rest from me trampling on his feet,' Tabitha said.

Archie protested while Jenny looked from one to the other, as if unsure what to say.

'I'll come back to you both soon, I promise,' Tabitha said. 'But I should really go and speak to Dr Collins and Captain Learman. I don't want them to think I'm ignoring them.'

She turned away and hurried off, skirts swishing as Archie looked longingly after her. He turned to Jenny.

'Would you like to dance, Miss Jenny?' He held out his hand and she accepted it, smiling.

'I'd love to dance, thank you, Mr Gingham.'

But as she approached the doctor and Jacob, Kitty and her new husband beat her to it, so she stopped, not wishing to interrupt. Within moments, Jacob noticed her and she swallowed hard as his gaze met hers.

Neither Dr Collins nor the happy couple were aware Tabitha was standing nearby and she sucked in her breath as she saw Jacob offer a brief apology before detaching himself from the group and walking towards her.

'Good evening, Tabitha,' he said, his deep, mellow voice.

'Good evening, Jacob.' She spoke softly and smiled up at him, wondering whether her guardian angel would truly guide her into marriage with the man she so loved.

'Do you still think we shouldn't dance together?' He spoke softly, too.

'I think it's best, but I'm sure the bride would be delighted to partner you.' She smiled mischievously at him.

'Tabitha, I think, as we cannot dance together, we should mingle. I'm noticing an occasional curious gaze as people dance past.' He bent to retrieve a blossom that had fallen from her hair. Instead of handing it to her, he reached out and slipped it behind one of her ears.

Swiftly, she bobbed him a curtsey.

'I'm indebted to you, Captain. I'm pleased you were able to come and congratulate the bride and groom.'

With that, she turned away and hurried back to where she'd been sitting. There was no sign of Jenny or Archie. Nor anyone else nearby whom she knew until Will Mackie appeared.

'May I sit beside you awhile, Miss Westwood?'

'Of course, Will. Don't Benjamin and Kitty look happy?'

'Aye, indeed they do. But did I catch you looking a little sad? You can tell me to mind my own beeswax if you wish!'

Tabitha shook her head.

'I'll do nothing of the sort. But I'm not feeling sad — only a little thoughtful.'

'Maybe you're thinking of your own wedding day? There's more than one young man around who admires you and that's a fact. It's possible you're thinking of one in particular ...'

Tabitha felt embarrassed though she knew Will Mackie would never wish that to happen.

'Um ... I'm still making my way in this new world, Will. I need to gain more teaching experience before I contemplate marriage, no matter who my husband might be.'

'An answer I'd have expected, knowing your way with words and your sensible outlook, but might I offer a word of warning?'

Before she could respond, she saw Jacob making his way through the groups of chatting people surrounding the dance floor. She shot to her feet, with Will almost as speedy.

'Jacob, what is it?'

'One of Edward's children is poorly. Flora asked a neighbour to ride here and inform him. Will, can you take the doctor and me back to the house, please? Miss Westwood, will you come, too? I'm sure Flora will be glad of your help. I'll return to Edward and see you both outside.' Jacob set off.

'I need to tell my missus before we go,' Will said. Tabitha followed Jacob.

'I'll see you outside, too, Will.'

As she left the party, Tabitha noticed a fair-haired girl in a corner, perched on Archie Gingham's knee. She wondered whether the warning Will was prevented

from giving her, could be connected with
the young couple in the corner.

Jealous Heart

The moment Will halted the pony, Edward jumped out, muttering an apology to the others.

'Don't be silly. Go to your family,' Jacob called before getting out and helping Tabitha on to the ground.

'I'll find Mrs Collins then come and tell you how things are,' Tabitha said, squeezing his arm.

It occurred to her how relaxed she was with Jacob now. Back in London, they wouldn't have enjoyed such freedom and lack of etiquette.

Inside, she headed for the children's room, halting outside the open door. There was no sign of Mrs Collins but her husband was bending over one of the twins and Tabitha couldn't see which. She tiptoed away and met Flora in the hallway.

'Mrs Collins, what can I do to help?'

'Thank you, Tabitha. If you could make a pot of tea, that would be very welcome. And see if Jacob would like a cup, please.

'Daisy has a fever and I've taken Edie into our room. She's asleep but I want to keep an eye on her as Edward thinks it likely she'll get whatever it is.'

'I'll make tea then, if you like, I'll sit with Edie in case she wakes up. You must take care of yourself, ma'am.'

'Thank you, but you're as bad as my husband! You're a good girl, Tabitha. Jacob has told Edward and me about your engagement and I'm happy for you both.'

'Rest assured I won't leave you for a while yet, Mrs Collins. If you'll still allow me to be the children's governess, that is.'

'There's no question about that, my dear. And while we're alone, you must call me Flora. Now I must go back.'

Tabitha went into the kitchen, her thoughts in a turmoil. Jacob appeared in the doorway.

'I heard you talking to Flora. I feel helpless — is there anything I can do to help?'

Tabitha was about to reply when Edward appeared in the doorway.

'Tabitha, could you assist me with my daughter? I need to sponge her with cool water to help reduce the fever and I need help to move her with as little disturbance as possible.'

'I'll bring water and cloths.' Tabitha sprang into action.

'I'll make tea for Flora,' Jacob said.

Edward looked from one to the other.

'Thank you, both of you.' He turned and left the room.

Tabitha shot an anguished look at Jacob. 'I can only imagine what this is like for him — for both of them. Dr Collins has the life of one of his children in his hands ...'

'We must all pray,' Jacob said. 'Call me if there's anything I can do.'

* * *

Next morning, Tabitha entered the kitchen, unsure how things were for the family. She'd been gently told to go to bed around midnight when Jacob informed her Edward intended sleeping on the floor beside Daisy's bed.

Muriel greeted Tabitha.

'Is there news of little Daisy? I've not long risen from my bed.'

'I know nothing, either, I'm afraid. Does all seem quiet on the family's side of the house?'

'Yes, I can't make up my mind whether to take tea to the mistress or not. What do you think?'

'She may not have got to sleep until the small hours. Perhaps it's best to wait a while.'

'I hope no news means good news,' Muriel said.

Tabitha was about to agree when Jacob appeared in the doorway. She still couldn't get used to seeing him without his seafaring beard. But she didn't mind whether he was clean-shaven or not. He was still Jacob, the man she loved with all her heart.

'Good morning, ladies,' he said. 'Is there any news?'

'Not yet, sir,' Muriel said.

'What time did you get to bed, Captain?' Tabitha asked.

'Close to two o'clock. Then I found it difficult to settle.'

'It's been a worrying time and we can only hope Daisy pulls through.' Tabitha moved across to the scullery. 'I'll brew a pot of tea and there's porridge simmering. Probably fresh eggs and bread — is that right, Muriel?'

'Oh, yes. Kitty would have my hide for a saddle if I didn't follow her good example.'

'Miss Westwood? Would you step outside with me for a while? As long as this doesn't inconvenience you, Muriel?'

'Not at all, sir. Nothing's going to spoil and if the master comes in, the tea will be brewed soon.' She shot Tabitha a meaningful glance.

Outside, Jacob took Tabitha's hand and drew her across the garden towards

Flora's flowerbed. Tabitha marvelled to see a large butterfly, jet black with king-fisher blue markings, seeking nectar amongst the bright blossoms.

'I wanted to say again, both Edward and Flora were glad to hear the news of our engagement, my dear. However, I think you'll agree, this isn't the time to consider our future while they have so much on their minds.'

'Yes, I think the same. We must think first about the family and leave our plans for now.'

He raised her hand to his lips and kissed it.

'Wise words. I'd expect nothing less of you. But there's something troubling me and I know you won't mind if I ask you about it.'

Tabitha frowned.

'Is it something I've said? I'd hate to think I've upset you, Jacob!'

'It's something I overheard last evening at the celebration. Two people were talk-ing about you as a possible bride for someone called Archie Gingham. Is he a relation of the farmer who Kitty's married to now?'

Tabitha felt her cheeks burn.

'Archie is Benjamin Gingham's son, yes. But there's no question of him being a possible match for me. I wish people wouldn't gossip!'

'I wasn't introduced, but was he the young man you were dancing with when Edward and I arrived?'

He looks so stern, Tabitha thought.

'That was Archie, yes.'

'A handsome young fellow and about your age, I think. One couldn't blame him for being smitten.'

'I cannot help his feelings, Jacob. Believe me, Archie hasn't been on my mind since you came to stay and I'm horrified to hear people are saying otherwise.'

To her dismay, Jacob dropped her hand as though it was in flames.

'Does that mean you were attracted to him whilst I was away from you all those months? Please be honest with me.'

She stared at him, her heart thumping

like a frightened bird's.

'I'd never lie to you, Jacob. You must know that. I might have wondered if something could come of my friendship with Archie, though I've seen very little of him. There was a time when I felt things were not to be between you and me. A time when I feared my status would prevent you from having anything more to do with me.'

All she could hear was birdsong. Jacob was staring at her as though she'd turned into a stranger.

'Surely you couldn't think that? From the moment I set eyes on you, I felt our lives were destined to be entwined. Did you not feel that, too? I thought we were of the same mind.'

This couldn't be happening! Tabitha's mouth dried so she could barely form the words to reassure him. Her world was falling apart because of a silly remark he'd overheard.

She tried to tell him how she'd seen Archie canoodling with her friend, Jenny and how she'd been relieved, but the power of speech had deserted her.

Jenny had liked the look of Archie that time she'd clapped eyes on him and Tabitha suspected Archie's feelings for her had never been exactly deep, having seen him with Jenny the night before. Why was Jacob speaking like this?

'I think we're both overwrought from worry and lack of sleep,' Tabitha said. 'You've heard something that's not true. Please believe me.'

But to her dismay, he turned away and strode back to the house.

Bad News

Tabitha hurried to her room to wash the tears from her face. She could hear voices and best of all, a peal of laughter that must have come from one of the twins. This made her smile, for as long as all was well, that was what really mattered. With all the hardships endured so far in her life, perhaps she'd been foolish to imagine a dream could come true.

As soon as she'd tidied herself, she put on a clean pinafore and went to the kitchen.

The doctor was there, speaking to Muriel. Little Edie was sitting at the kitchen table, eating bread and jam. There was no sign of Flora or Daisy. As for Jacob, he was probably packing his bag, having decided he never wanted to set eyes on Tabitha again.

She walked towards Edward Collins and as he turned towards her, she thought he looked tired, but that wasn't unusual for the only doctor for miles around.

'I want to thank you for your help last night, Tabitha. Also, I want to apologise for being a little unwelcoming towards you when you first arrived.'

'Please, Dr Collins, you've nothing to apologise for, but tell me, please, how Daisy is this morning, and your wife, of course?'

He beamed.

'I'm pleased to say Daisy's out of danger and sleeping normally now. Children's ailments are often not as serious as one might fear, but their constitutions make them vulnerable, of course. My wife has hardly left her side so I'm sure Edie will be glad to have your company today, as long as you're not too tired to carry out your duties.'

The little girl smiled shyly as Tabitha assured her employer all was well. Unless, she thought, you counted a broken heart. For Jacob had seemed so angry when they were talking in the garden. It was as though he'd been a tinderbox waiting to flare!

And she daren't even ask after him, as the doctor had enough to worry about. Maybe he'd even be relieved to know his friend wasn't intending to whisk the children's governess away after all. Who knew?

Tabitha only knew if Jacob decided to break their engagement, she would never, ever, consider marriage to any other man.

She pulled herself back to the moment, as Edward told Muriel he'd join his guest in the dining-room for breakfast. Tabitha, stifling a sob, began eating her porridge, listening to Edie, who appeared to have become almost as chatty as her twin now she had their governess to herself. Half-listening, she wondered how Jacob felt now and whether he'd seek her out later. She desperately wanted to reassure him properly, having been too shocked earlier when he voiced his feelings so unexpectedly.

Lessons began. Soon, Tabitha became

aware of Will Mackie's arrival and the sound of masculine voices followed by silence, so Tabitha supposed both the doctor and his guest must have gone to town together.

The hours passed. Muriel took food and drink to Flora and Daisy, while Tabitha kept Edie amused, reading to her after lunch. Soon, Edie's eyelids were drooping and Tabitha draped a shawl over her and tiptoed from the room. The house seemed quiet but she felt no desire for company. There was only one person she longed to see.

Tabitha had no way of knowing what the captain might decide and it irked her that he could be so careless of her feelings. It was so unlike his usual manner, yet how did she know anything, given her lack of knowledge regarding the masculine character?

By late afternoon, Flora was in the parlour spending time with Edie, while Daisy slept again, Tabitha beside her, reading a book. Sounds from outside floated through the open window as Will returned, bringing, she presumed, his two passengers. She heard the sounds of the pony trotting away and the rumble of the wheels fade into the distance but couldn't detect any more conversation.

It was none of her business what Jacob did, but she wondered whether he'd been spending time in town, discussing possible houses or plots of land suitable for creating his dream. Was she still part of that dream?

Hearing a tap on the bedroom door, Tabitha jumped to her feet and went into the hallway. The doctor's expression was so serious, she stared at him, fearful of what he might say.

'I'm afraid Jacob is not very well. Not well at all.'

'Where … where is he, doctor?'

'In the hospital. I thought it best to take him there as he complained of certain symptoms to me as we were waiting for Will to collect us from the hotel. I have concerns over Jacob having contracted some illness while on his ship. There's so much we have to learn about these different maladies and how to treat them.'

'I'm afraid this might be my fault!'

'Why do you say that?' He was looking at her in puzzlement. 'Has something happened? I only ask because Flora and I are fond of you both, you know. We don't want to lose you, but we rejoice for Jacob and his wife to be.'

His kind remark brought tears to Tabitha's eyes.

'Thank you, but we had a disagreement yesterday evening. Jacob was angry because he heard silly gossip about Archie Gingham and me being fond of one another.'

Edward Collins looked thoughtful.

'That doesn't sound like Jacob, which makes me think his outburst was connected with whatever ails him. I'll return to the hospital after supper and see how he is.

'Meanwhile, we should keep ourselves to ourselves as well as we can. This doesn't necessarily mean Jacob's malady is the same as Daisy's. Nor does it mean that anyone else in the household is bound to be affected.

'If Jacob knew how upset you were, he would, I'm sure, be saddened. Have you any message for him? Better still, could you write a note for me to hand to him?'

Tabitha hurried away to find paper, pen and ink, praying her beloved would be in a fit state to read her message.

My darling. How can I find words to express my sorrow on hearing of your illness? I hope, by the time this letter reaches you, you feel well enough to read it. Ever since we parted last night, I have felt saddened, knowing, although I never intended it, I have caused you distress.

Please believe me, Jacob, when I say that during the time when I never dared hope your feelings for me might match my own, I showed only courtesy and friendliness towards Archie Gingham.

Nothing untoward ever took place between us and indeed, it was a relief to me when I saw him with my friend Jenny at the wedding celebration.

There is no other man in the world for me but you, Jacob. I offer you my whole-hearted love and devotion for as long as we are granted. For I truly believe, as you do, we are destined to be together.

With sincere wishes for your speedy recovery,

Your loving fiancée,

Tabitha

Happy is the Bride

'Good day, Muriel, am I the first one up?' Tabitha stood in the kitchen doorway.

'Mr Mackie drove the doctor off to town just a short while back.' Muriel carried on kneading dough. 'I'm sorry to hear of the captain's illness. You must be sick with worry. Help yourself to tea.'

'I'm sure we all hope he pulls through. Not just me.' She poured her tea.

Muriel looked around.

'Just checking for little 'uns with big ears. I do know you and the captain have an understanding, my dear.'

Tabitha gasped.

'How on earth ...?'

'How do you think?'

'Kitty? Kitty always knows everything.'

'That's as maybe but she doesn't gossip. Nor do I, in case you're wondering. I remembered the captain in my prayers

214

last night, and the Doctor, too. They're both good men.'

The morning flew by. Tabitha tried her best to concentrate on helping Edie with her lessons, now and then picturing Jacob's handsome face, especially those eyes, deep blue and seeming to look right through to her soul.

After the midday meal, everyone took a rest, though Daisy was complaining about being stuck indoors. Still the doctor remained absent.

'Edward's often out all day,' Flora reminded Tabitha when they met later. 'That doesn't mean you've reason to worry about Jacob.'

'I so wish I could visit him.'

'I doubt they'd allow that, my dear. When my husband returns, I'm sure we'll find out how the patient is. Meanwhile, thank you so much for the way you're coping with everything. Edward told me how calm you were while he was trying to bring down Daisy's fever.'

'I was only doing what anyone would have done.'

Jacob was such a good man and it was a relief to know the real reason for his sudden suspicious, cold manner. It hadn't been her Jacob speaking those words, but a Jacob attacked by illness. She managed a smile.

'I'll take Edie down to the shore, shall I?'

'She'll enjoy that.' Flora smiled. 'And try not to worry, Tabitha. Take heart and remember Jacob's in good hands.'

Much to her relief, Tabitha was summoned to the parlour that evening as soon as the doctor returned.

'He's suffering from cholera,' Edward said, holding up his hand as the women gasped. 'It could be far worse and he's fortunate he mentioned his symptoms as soon as he noticed something was wrong.

'He needs to stay in hospital so we can keep an eye on him, but as he's still a relatively young man with a strong constitution, I see no reason why he shouldn't recover in a week or so.'

'Are we at risk of catching it, too?'

Flora asked.

'I don't think so, my dear. I've always instructed our staff in matters of hygiene and I'm satisfied both Kitty and now Muriel keep good standards. It's possible Jacob contracted the disease while still on his ship.'

'Is it coincidence that Daisy became poorly?' Tabitha asked.

'Yes. Daisy's illness isn't connected to his and she seems to have recovered quickly. I'm keeping an eye on Edie, though I'm hoping she escapes being ill.' Edward turned to her.

'I handed your note to Jacob, but advised him not to write a reply, though with his illness, it's believed to be spread by contaminated food or water. This convinces me he contracted the disease on board ship.'

Tabitha, though relieved to hear Jacob wasn't in grave danger, wanted to ask a very important question.

'Forgive me, Doctor, but did he ask if he could write to me?'

'Yes. You may of course write another

note to him, if you wish.'

Tabitha bit her lip, not wishing to be a nuisance. Luckily Flora came to her rescue.

'Edward,' she said, 'the poor girl wants to be assured her fiancé misses her! Can you not put her out of her misery?'

Tabitha held her breath. Edward cleared his throat.

'I'm much better advising patients about defects of the heart rather than matters of the heart. Jacob's face lit up when I handed him your letter, Tabitha, and after reading it, I needed to look away as he turned his head away from me ...'

'Go on,' Flora said. 'You're doing very well — for a man.'

Edward stared at the window.

'He, um, he told me he didn't know how he'd manage being unable to see you until he left hospital. Also, he said he'd behaved very impolitely to you after the wedding celebration and asked me to say he'll make it up to you. And, oh yes, he said he, um ... he loves you very much.'

Tabitha managed to stammer out her thanks before bursting into tears.

'You're trembling,' Flora said, putting a reassuring arm around Tabitha's shoulder.

Tabitha gulped.

'I think it must be relief. I've been suffering agonies. I thought I'd upset him so badly that he'd decide not to speak to me ever again.'

Flora chuckled.

'Lovers' tiffs — they're understandable and even more so now we know Jacob wasn't his usual self.'

'I hated quarrelling. I hope it never happens again.'

'It probably will, my dear. But you should both be aware of the importance of saying sorry when you know you're in the wrong. Jacob has shown how admirable and sincere a man he is. I think you're well suited, you two. But I hope you don't marry until after this baby is born, else how shall I dance at your wedding?'

On the day Jacob was allowed to leave hospital, Tabitha could hardly contain herself when the pony and trap pulled up outside. Will Mackie jumped down as she hurried forward, his kindly face splitting into a grin.

'Someone's very pleased to see the captain,' he teased. 'I wonder why! My that's a pretty blush, Miss Westwood.'

She didn't care whether her cheeks told tales, so relieved was she to see Jacob again.

'Hello, Tabitha.' Jacob smiled down at her then clambered to the ground.

Will reached for Jacob's bag and headed for the front door.

'Let's take a walk around the garden,' Jacob said. 'Or are you in the middle of a lesson?'

'I can spare a few minutes. The girls are in the kitchen with Muriel.'

He reached for her hand and drew her close. Tabitha felt as though her heart might burst with love.

'I can't apologise enough for the way

I treated you after the wedding. Can you ever forgive me?'

'There's nothing to forgive. You were unwell and not seeing things straight. The important thing is you're better now.'

He bent his head. His kiss was tender. His arms around her made her feel safe and loved. But how long would it be before he left Australia again? As if reading her mind, Jacob stroked her bright hair lovingly.

'I've had a lot of time to think and I want to ask you a question.'

'What question is this?'

'Will you marry me, Tabitha?'

She laughed.

'You know I'll marry you, Jacob. I said yes the first time and I'm saying it again now.'

He took her hand and led her across the garden to a sheltered spot.

'How wonderful it is to be in the fresh air, hearing the birdsong and seeing the colourful flowers.' He took both her hands in his. 'I mean will you marry me before I return to London?

'I don't think I can bear the thought of sailing there and back unless I know my wife is waiting for my return. I only wish you could accompany me, but I believe you'll be safer here. I don't like the thought of you being on board with the risk of illness occurring.'

She nestled against him.

'But I feel the same about you! If only you didn't have to go back.'

'I need to deal with some personal matters and when I return, we may be able to move into our new home.'

She gasped.

'So soon? How can this be?'

'Before my illness, I made certain arrangements. Edward knows all about it and he'll consult you about matters on which he thinks you should express an opinion. We could marry at the little church near the town hall,' he continued. 'Can you arrange for a dress to be made without delay?'

'I expect Flora will help me, if you're sure this is what you want.'

'It's what I want more than anything else in the world, my angel.'

* * *

'So soon?' Jacob and Tabitha stood in the parlour with the doctor and his wife. 'Well, congratulations to you both,' Flora said. 'Though I'm not sure we should forgive you, Jacob, for stealing our governess!'

Jacob chuckled, his arm around Tabitha's waist.

'Don't worry, she's not deserting you yet.'

'I'm pleased to remain as the children's governess,' Tabitha said, 'but we hope the twins will continue their lessons when we start our school.'

'We're aware they lack the company of other children,' Edward said, 'and when our third child's old enough, I hope you'll accept him or her into the school, too.'

'At the moment I'm more concerned about the wedding!' Flora said. 'We must arrange for your dress to be made, Tabitha. Shall I do that for you?'

'Yes, please. I intend carrying on with the children's lessons meanwhile.'

The doctor glanced at his wife.

'I've said it before, but Tabitha's worth her weight in gold.'

'And I couldn't have better employers, or pupils. I should be honoured if you'd give me away, Edward.'

'I wanted him to be my best man, but I'll stand back,' Jacob said. 'If we time things right, I can ask one of my brother officers. The ship I'm to take back to London docks in a few days' time.'

'Excellent. I'd be honoured to give you away, Tabitha.'

She was torn between happiness over marrying Jacob and sadness, knowing he must leave her soon afterwards.

Later that day, Flora whisked her away to the dressmaker while Jacob took the twins for a walk. He'd been pronounced fit to return to his duties so there weren't many days left in which to arrange the marriage.

'I don't care about a party, but does it

worry you?' Jacob asked later while they sat in the garden.

'Not at all. We could always have one once you're back for good.'

He kissed her hand.

'I look forward to that day.'

'Not as much as I do!' She chuckled. 'Do you realise, we wouldn't be allowed to see each other in private like this, if we were in England?'

'Remember how the padre gently put me right when he insisted on sitting with you during your reading sessions? It hadn't occurred to me people might think my motives were, well, ungentlemanly.'

'He was very kind. But so were you, and if anyone had said anything about you to my face, I think Jenny would have punched them!'

He hugged her to him.

'I'd forgotten about your friend and how you first met. Would you like her to be your maid of honour?'

Tabitha shook her head.

'I thought about it but decided not.

I hope she'll join our celebrations later in the year, but I've asked Flora if the twins could accompany me down the aisle. This is a very private wedding and I think it's better not to involve too many people.'

A few days later, Tabitha set off for church with the doctor and his family. Jacob had spent the night before his wedding at the hotel used by the shipping company and he'd been joined there by his best man. On arrival at the church, Tabitha was surprised to find a small knot of folk gathered, one of whom she saw was Jenny.

Her friend rushed over to kiss her when she alighted from the doctor's trap. 'I couldn't stay away! Don't you look beautiful in that blue gown!'

'I'm delighted to see you, Jenny, but how in the world did you know?'

'Muriel couldn't resist telling her sister and Kitty told Mr Gingham and he told Archie, who told me! I know in the beginning he was sweet on you, Tabby, but I had a feeling you'd lost yer heart to the captain. And,' she said shyly, 'Archie and me might be following you two up the aisle one of these days!'

How could Tabitha possibly send her away?

'You're very welcome. We decided to postpone our wedding breakfast until after Jacob retires from voyaging. You and Archie will receive an invitation then, never fear.'

Edward cleared his throat.

'Tabitha, it's time we went in. Your bridegroom and his best man are waiting.' He offered her his arm.

The twins beamed at the bride, each girl clutching a small posy.

'Thank you, Edward, for all your kindness.' Tabitha hoped her mother and father were looking down on their daughter on her wedding day. 'Let's go and find Jacob.'

Love Letters

After waving her husband off at the quayside two days later, Tabitha knew the only way to survive this separation was to work hard. Or, even harder than usual. He'd taken her to see the land which he'd purchased and which was only a half-hour's walk from the doctor's house. There was a grove of trees nearby and plenty of ground for growing their own vegetables.

Tabitha knew nothing about building but she wasn't afraid to ask questions and the workmen grew accustomed to her turning up, writing notes and making little sketches.

They weren't to know these would help keep her husband informed of progress when she wrote him her next letter.

The family's anticipated happy event occurred one stormy night when Flora gave birth to a baby boy. Henry Jacob entered the world, red-faced and bawling, much to the delight and relief of his proud parents. Tabitha was touched when she and Jacob were asked to be the new baby's godparents.

Again, days and weeks turned into months. Tabitha, using the list of ports and dates Jacob had given her, timed her correspondence so when The Lady Gwendoline tied up at the next port of call, her letter would await him. In his turn, he wrote to her and through these expressions of love, each grew to know more about the other.

My darling Tabitha,

I know I'm asking a lot of my lawyer and my family, but you'll understand, my love, how much I long to return to you and to begin our new life together. What good news about Edward and Flora's little son! They must be so very proud. Please convey my congratulations, dear Tabitha. One day, my love, God willing, we too will know the joy of welcoming a son or daughter into our lives.

Tabitha, seated at the kitchen table, pressed his letter against her cheek after reading those words.

Jacob's next letter was written from Baker Street in London on February 14, 1866.

My darling Tabitha,

I write to you on St Valentine's Day. I have no pretty card to send, but through this letter, will try to communicate my loving feelings towards you, my dear wife. It gives me much joy to address you as such.

As you can see, I'm at my brother's house and pleased to report he and his family are well. They are delighted to learn of our marriage and send congratulations and best wishes for our future health and happiness.

Thank you for the letters I've found waiting for me at the ports. I like to hear about your busy days and to know the men are making progress with our new house.

I pray that the ocean will be kind when I make my final voyage for the company next Thursday. It's fitting, I think that I shall be taking over my last command on The Lady Gwendoline — a vessel you know I am fond of and which I reckon should go down in history as the ship where Captain Jacob Learman first met Miss Tabitha Westwood.

Please count the months from Saturday the 17th of February, my angel. For by the time you receive this letter, I shall be well on my way back to you. I hope the postal services as well as the seas look kindly upon us and that we continue to keep in touch until I return and take you in my arms as I so long to do.

Your loving husband,
Jacob

Together at Last

Tabitha was counting the days until *The Lady Gwendoline* was due to dock in Fairclough. She could only use an approximate date and knew how tides and prevailing winds affected the ship's progress.

One Saturday morning in August, Tabitha was only just dressed when she heard a banging on the back door. She hurried to open it but Muriel was already there.

'What's all this noise, Mr Mackie? You'd better have a good reason!'

'I have, Mrs Taylor.' His gaze moved to Tabitha. 'I know it's early, but the missus and me thought you'd want to know, lass.'

'Goodness! What's happened, Will?'

'Himself's been sighted along the coast! Your man's bringing in *The Lady Gwendoline* — I was feeding the chooks when my neighbour came back from night fishing and told me he'd seen the ship and got out his telescope to see which one it was.'

Muriel gasped and clapped her hands. Tabitha stood beside her, too stunned to speak. Muriel put her arms round her.

'D'you hear what he says? What wonderful news, Tabitha!'

'I didn't expect him until next week. Oh, my goodness. When do you think he'll reach Fairclough, Will?'

'In an hour or so, I reckon. With the doctor's permission, I can drive you there so the captain sees you waiting on the quayside.'

Sensible, practical Muriel almost choked and Tabitha realised she was overcome with emotion. She, however, remained strangely calm.

'That would mean so much to me, but my duties …'

She was interrupted as the doctor came in.

'Good man, Will. Yes, please take Mrs Learman down to the quayside. He'll be kept busy for a while, won't he, Tabitha?'

She nodded, suddenly overcome with the reality of Jacob's nearness.

'Thank you,' she said. 'He can probably see me for a few minutes but there's always a lot for the captain to oversee before leaving his ship.'

Tabitha hurried back to her room. Her fingers trembled as she found a jacket, knowing the morning air would be chilly. But her husband was coming home to her. And once more her life was about to change.

When she returned to the kitchen, Muriel had made tea.

'Drink that and there's a chunk of bread and honey. I need to go to my room. Won't be long!'

Gratefully, Tabitha sipped the hot brew. She felt too excited now to eat but knew better than not to make an attempt. Before long, Muriel appeared, holding a dark red velvet cape in her arms.

'Never mind that jacket — I want you to wear this.'

'It's beautiful, Muriel, but why? I won't

touch it for fear my fingers are sticky.'

'You can wash them in a moment. I want you to wear my cloak because I wore it on my wedding day. For all I go on about men's cranky ways, I was a happy girl when I got married. And I'd like the captain to see you when he's heading into port — your beautiful hair loose and all.' She hung the cloak on the back of a chair.

* * *

Jacob felt a mixture of elation and wistfulness as he guided *The Lady Gwendoline* towards harbour. In the distance he could see the scattered buildings of Fairclough and drawing closer, he blinked hard, unsure whether he was imagining things. Slowly, the vessel moved through the water towards her berth. And on the quayside, stood no apparition, but his darling wife. Her glorious coppery hair blowing in the breeze, she wore a ruby-red cloak over her neat grey gown.

Jacob felt a surge of emotion. His first

reaction was to let his lieutenant take over the wheel — the man was perfectly capable — but the captain remained in position, knowing Tabitha would understand how on this last voyage, he wanted to retain command until the end.

He raised one hand in salute and before long, the ship was berthed and its captain released to make his way to the gangway.

'I'll be back soon,' he called to his second-in-command before hurtling down from the bridge. Sailors made way for him. The gangway was barely in position when he jumped on and hurried along it, to land on the quayside.

'Tabitha!'

She was standing some distance away, but as soon as she saw him safely on the dockside, she started running forward, as he sprinted towards her. The mischievous breeze sent her hair flying out and her cloak streaming behind her. She'd never looked so beautiful to him and he knew he would hold that image in his mind and in his heart for the rest of his life.

He lifted her off her feet and whirled her round, each of them laughing and Tabitha squealing for mercy! Jacob placed her gently down, folded her into his embrace and kissed her, much to the delight of his sailors who began cheering and whistling, causing Mrs Learman's cheeks to turn a becoming shade of pink.

At last he let her go and stood, holding both her hands.

'I never in my wildest dreams thought you'd be here to greet me,' he whispered at last. He hugged her. 'I have to go, but I'll see you soon. If Will's busy, I can find someone to bring me to you.'

'I doubt Mr Mackie will let that happen.' She smiled. 'Edward says he'll reserve a room for us at the hotel tonight, but everyone will want to see you, of course.'

'I owe so much to my friends,' Jacob said. 'What progress has been made on our house, darling girl?'

'That must stay secret until we visit it. We could walk there this afternoon, if you're not too weary.'

'How could I possibly feel weary with my arms around my beautiful wife?'

She nestled against him and he kissed her again.

'Now, we can properly plan our future.'

Momentous News

One afternoon, a couple of months after Jacob and Tabitha moved into their new house, which they named Learman's Croft, Muriel visited.

'I've brought you a letter,' she announced as Tabitha took her into the kitchen.

'My goodness! Who on earth is writing to me?'

'Maybe you'll find out if you open it.' Muriel sat down while Tabitha filled the kettle. 'Whoever it is has addressed it to Miss Tabitha Westwood.'

'I'll open it in a while, but first tell me how you're all getting on. I haven't seen the doctor and his wife this week.' She busied herself with cups and plates. 'You know our very first term begins soon? Are the twins looking forward to it?'

Muriel laughed.

'If they had their way, they'd come and

board with you.'

'It'll be good for the twins to learn with other children.

'We've only five names on our books as yet, but I'm hoping folk will recommend us once they realise how serious we are about our pupils' progress.' She put a plate of oaten biscuits on the table.

'Cinnamon, like your recipe says.'

'Good girl. Anyone can see you're happy.'

Tabitha beamed.

'More than I'd ever imagined.' She poured tea. 'Now to see what this says.' She ripped open the envelope, frowning as she scanned the writing.

This was a momentous thing to happen and much as she was fond of Muriel, she wanted Jacob to be the first to learn her news. She folded the letter again and put it in her apron pocket.

Muriel glanced at the clock on the wall.

'I must go soon. I hope you've not received bad news, my dear. You know you can trust me if you need someone to talk to.'

'I do. Thank you, Muriel, but I need time to let this news sink in.'

Muriel smiled.

'Well, you know where I am. I got a ride over with Mr Mackie but the walk back will do me good. Where's the captain today?'

'Working in the schoolroom. Best we don't disturb him.'

'You're a hard taskmaster.' Muriel grinned. 'Be sure to give him my kindest regards.'

'Of course I will.' Tabitha hugged Muriel, waved her off and hurried into the schoolroom, using the door from the side passage.

Jacob was banging a nail into the wall behind the teacher's desk. A framed map of Australia waited to be hung.

'Was that Muriel I heard?' He reached for his wife's hand and kissed it. 'I'm dusty and thirsty. Will you take pity on a poor workman?'

She ruffled the beard he'd decided to keep until term began.

'There's tea in the pot and I have news from England. Come through to the kitchen.'

Jacob read the letter slowly before looking up.

'So, I'm married to an heiress?'

'I can't believe my grandmother left me her house and most of her money. I've not heard one word from her — even since I wrote, telling her I was engaged to be married.'

'Again, I put Edward and Flora's address at the top of the page.'

'From what you've said, she probably had a guilty conscience.'

'I'm sorry to hear of her death, but it's impossible for me to travel to Lancashire. Nor am I used to having lots of money. My goodness, Jacob, whatever am I to do?'

'I understand you've had a shock, my darling, but I'm convinced your mother and father would be pleased for you.'

'For us, Jacob.'

He nodded.

'And from the letter, we know Mrs

Pinkerton is still in residence, with the cook.'

'Yes, Alice worked for my grandmother for years. Pinkerton and her get on and I trust them to take good care of the house.'

'I have a good lawyer in London, but I see no reason why you shouldn't request your grandmother's lawyer to act on your behalf. Why not write to Mrs Pinkerton and to Alice, asking them what they intend to do? You'll want to let the property, I'm sure.'

She stared back at him.

'I can't push my grandma's employees out of their home. It may not be so easy for them to find another position at their ages.'

'It's not impossible that tenants might keep them on. Meanwhile, you'll need to ask the lawyer to arrange for wages to be paid regularly to each of them until such time as they either leave or become employed by the new tenants.'

'Thank goodness I'm married to you and not dealing with this alone.

But Jacob, I've just realised, if our new school proves to be successful, we'll be able to use the money I've inherited, to build not just another classroom, but a separate school building!'

One Year Later

Tabitha was sitting with Flora in the parlour of the Collins's house. She finished explaining what troubled her then sat back and sighed.

'Dear Tabitha, you've had such a lot on your mind for months now. No wonder you're concerned all isn't well with you. But it seems to me this is no problem, but rather a blessing! You need to see Edward so he may examine you.' She paused and smiled mischievously. 'Can you truly not guess what's happening?' She patted her waistline.

Tabitha gasped.

'Really? You think I might be ...'

'Expecting a baby? Yes, I think it's highly possible, but I think you should see Edward as soon as he returns, then you can go home and tell Jacob your good news. Will shall drive you, even though you insisted on walking here.'

Tabitha still felt bemused.

'I do so hope you're right, Flora. Jacob will be so very delighted. Between you and me, I thought perhaps there might be something wrong with me.'

Flora rose and put her arms around her.

'He'll not want you to go on teaching, will he? Not if I know Jacob.'

'If I am with child, we'll advertise for another teacher as soon as possible. Jacob has already spoken of the possibility of employing a British couple. He thinks there will be more free settlers coming here in future.'

'It's true there's a big need for people with all kinds of skills to settle here. I hope you'll go on working for a few months longer though. My girls will be so sad to lose their favourite teacher.'

'I shan't tell Jacob that!'

'You make an excellent team.' She raised one hand. 'I can hear them coming up the drive. Edward's been to the hospital to check on a patient. Before long, you'll know whether I'm proved right in my diagnosis, or not!'

To Tabitha's delight, Edward confirmed she was indeed expecting a child. He gave her some advice, told her to ask Flora if she'd any queries, as his wife was well-qualified to answer them, having borne three children.

Will Mackie drove her home. Jacob was sitting outside on the veranda, reading a book, when the pony and trap came through the gate. He rose and came to meet his wife.

'Thanks, Will. Give my regards to your lady wife, would you?'

'I will, Captain.'

They watched him drive off. Tabitha linked her arm in his and led him back into the house.

'I have something of interest to tell you.'

'What's all this about?' He smiled down at her.

'I think I might make you guess! Sit down.'

He did what she said then pulled her on to his lap. She snuggled against him.

'Well, well. Flora's found us someone suitable to help teach at the school?'

'Not yet, but she's doing her best. Try again.'

He looked wary.

'She's not … Flora isn't expecting another child, is she?'

'No, but you're getting warmer.'

'Tabitha? What are you saying?' He held her away from him, pushing a stray coppery lock away from her face.

'I'm saying you're going to be a father, Jacob. Edward has examined me and confirms I'm with child.'

'What did you say?'

Patiently, she broke the news again.

'He can't be absolutely certain, but he thinks the baby's due in six and a half months' time.'

She stopped talking as Jacob held her close again.

'On our wedding day, I thought I was the most fortunate man in the world. Now you've convinced me all over again!'